The Boy Allies In The Baltic

Robert L. Drake

THE BOY ALLIES IN THE BALTIC

CHAPTER I.

ON A RAID.

"Submerge to five fathoms, Mr. Templeton!"

The speaker was Lord Hastings, commander of the British submarine D-17.

Jack Templeton, a British youth and first officer of the under-sea craft, repeated the command for which he had been waiting now for some moments.

"Mr. Chadwick!"

Lord Hastings' voice again.

"Sir!"

A third figure, standing upon the bridge — now enclosed as the submarine sank from the surface — came to attention before his commander. Frank Chadwick, an American youth and second officer of the vessel, awaited instructions.

"Everything shipshape?" questioned his commander sharply.

"Yes, sir. Engine-room trouble all repaired, sir."

"Lookout posted forward?"

"Yes, sir!"

"Very well. Ten fathoms, Mr. Templeton!"

Lord Hastings turned from the periscope, through which he had been peering, and for a moment gazed thoughtfully at his two young officers before speaking. At last he said:

"Unless something goes wrong we will be in Heligoland within two hours!"

A startling statement, this, to one who did not know the nature of the man who made it; for it was a fact known to all the world that Heligoland, the great German fortress that guarded the approach to the few miles of German seacoast, was one of the strongest in the world — perhaps as well fortified as Gibraltar itself, and considered by naval experts equally as impregnable.

Apparently the D-17 was bent upon a perilous venture.

Such, indeed, was the case. The D-17, sister ship to the D-16, in which Lord Hastings and his two young officers had seen many exciting adventures, as related in "THE BOY ALLIES WITH THE TERROR OF THE SEAS," had left the coast of England the day before, heading straight for the strongly fortified German base; and now she was almost there.

Just what object Lord Hastings had in view neither Jack nor Frank knew, for Lord Hastings had not yet taken them fully into his confidence concerning this expedition. Since leaving England he had been busy in his cabin almost continuously poring over papers and maps, but both lads had a pretty shrewd idea that the venture was an important one.

Now Frank asked:

"And what are we going to do in there, sir?"

Lord Hastings smiled.

"What would be your idea about that?"

"Well," said Frank, "there are several things we might do. First, we might sink a couple of German war vessels. We might try and learn the lay of the land — perhaps I should say the water — or we might try and get ashore and so learn other matters of importance. Have I hit it, sir?"

"You have," returned his commander dryly; "you've hit it in more ways than one. In fact, I may say you have guessed shrewdly all through."

"Then I can do a little guessing, too," declared Jack.

"Well?" said Lord Hastings inquiringly.

"Well," said Jack, "we first shall probably make an attempt to get ashore, for there we can learn more than we could reconnoitering beneath the water. That's where we shall try to find our information. And we shall sink a couple of the enemy on our way out. Am I right, sir?"

"You are," replied Lord Hastings briefly, and turning on his heel he left the bridge and disappeared in his cabin, only to reappear a few moments later, charts and papers in his hands, announcing:

"Mr. Chadwick, you will take the wheel yourself. I'll stand beside you and give my orders. These waters are thickly strewn with mines and we can afford to take no chances."

Frank obeyed this command without question and Lord Hastings took his place beside him, first remarking to Jack:

"You will relieve the lookout forward, Mr. Templeton, and keep your eyes open. I need not mention the need of prompt action should you perceive danger ahead. Slow down to five knots!"

"Very well, sir."

Jack saluted, and after giving the command that reduced the speed of the vessel, took himself forward.

There, at the extreme bow, he relieved a sailor and took the watch himself.

Now the D-17, like her sister ship the D-16, which had been sunk off the Dardanelles – an accident in which all on board escaped as by a miracle – was as unlike other under-water craft as day is from night.

In the first place, she was able to remain under water indefinitely. It was not necessary for her to return to the surface every so often to replenish her air tanks, for she carried no tanks. The D-17 generated her air supply from the water, by means of a secret process known only to high officials of the British admiralty. Also, the D-17 was the last word in submarine craft in other respects. She had a speed of more than thirty knots when submerged, could move along even faster upon the surface of the water, and her bow, a solid piece of substantial glass, in which reposed a huge searchlight, made it possible for her to pick her course under the water – something that no other submarine craft was able to do. For this latter reason she could venture places where no other vessel would dare.

The huge light flashing in front now, Jack took his stand and stood with eyes straining into the distance ahead.

And while the D-17 is thus moving toward the strongest fortification of the enemy, a few words concerning the two subordinate officers aboard are necessary.

Frank Chadwick, an American youth of some seventeen years of age, found himself in his present position as a result of a series of strange happenings. He had lost his father in Italy immediately after the outbreak of the great war, and while hunting him in Naples, had been shanghaied aboard an Italian schooner. Here, following a mutiny of the crew and the death of the captain, he found himself a prisoner, remaining so until released by Jack Templeton.

The latter's appearance came about in this manner: Jack, the son of an Englishman, nevertheless had spent most of his life in a little African coast town. His father died there and Jack found himself sole owner of a little store, which had almost a native trade alone, though an occasional ship put in for supplies.

One day a schooner hove in sight. A boat put over the side and its occupants obtained provisions at Jack's store. In the lad's absence, they departed without making payment. Jack hurried after them to collect and climbed aboard the schooner just as she raised anchor. A fight followed his demand for payment. By some resourcefulness and some good hard fighting, the lad succeeded in gaining the upper hand. Then he released Frank, whom he found a prisoner with another, a British secret service agent.

A series of subsequent events threw the lads into the company of Lord Hastings, who, taking a liking to them, answered their pleas to be made sailors by securing them commissions and taking them aboard his own ship at the opening of the great world war.

Then had followed months of excitement and adventure. They had taken part in British successes and reverses on all the seven seas. They had been "in at the death" in the first British naval victory off Heligoland; they had followed the German cruiser Emden, "the Terror of the Sea"; they had been in action with the British fleet that destroyed the German squadron off the

Falkland Islands in the western hemisphere; they had seen action in other parts of the globe—at the Dardanelles, with the Japanese at Tsingchau, with the French in the Adriatic and with the Russians in the Baltic.

In a word, they were veterans.

Many were the narrow escapes they had had, but they had always survived. Their latest venture had almost cost Frank his life, for, after the submarine upon which they sailed had been destroyed, Frank engaged in a death struggle with a British traitor in the waters of the North Sea and had won by a scant fraction. He was unconscious when rescued by his chum and he had remained inactive, as had the others, in England for several weeks.

But now, the D-17 having been put in service, Lord Hastings had been named to command her and all were eager to get busy again.

Frank, though sturdy and strong, was by no means a match for his chum, a powerful and husky young Englishman. Also he was naturally more hot-headed than his friend, and given to taking foolhardy chances—at times. Jack's coolness had saved both more than once.

Jack was what Frank called a real fighter and had proved his mettle more than once since the two had been together. Strong as an ox, he was a bad customer to tackle in a rough and tumble and he was exceedingly proficient in the use of his fists. Also he was a fair swordsman and a fair shot.

It was in the latter accomplishment that Frank excelled. He was a dead shot with either rifle or revolver, as he had proved in several tight situations where straight shooting had been necessary. He had never failed in this respect.

Fortunately, both lads spoke German and French as well as English, and under Lord Hastings' tutoring, they had also picked up a smattering of Italian, Russian and Hungarian—not much, perhaps, but enough to carry on a conversation, although with some difficulty.

At the time the D-17 made her way toward Heligoland, the great war was almost at a standstill. It seemed that the warring nations had reached a deadlock that could not be broken.

On sea, of course, the Allies held the whip hand, except for the submarine warfare instigated by the Central Powers. This, however, due in a measure to the activities of British under-sea craft upon which Jack and Frank had served, had been somewhat lessened lately and German U-boats, as they had come to be known, had not been so active recently.

On land, however, it seemed that neither side had gained much in the last few months. What advantage there was seemed to have rested with the Germans, for the Kaiser's mighty drive through the Balkans had completely crushed heroic little Serbia and had opened a path to Constantinople for the German hordes. Also it had brought Bulgaria into the war on the side of the Central Powers, giving them the armed weight necessary to keep Greece and Roumania from throwing their support to the Allies, much as they would have liked to do so.

This was the situation, then, when the D-17 steamed slowly toward the German naval fortress of Heligoland.

As Lord Hastings, standing by Frank at the wheel, gave the course, avoiding mines as well as he could by the chart that had somehow come into his possession, Jack retained his place forward in the glass-like cage, his eyes steadily ahead.

For an hour, perhaps, he sat there, seeing nothing that indicated danger.

Then, suddenly, his right hand shot out, his finger touched a little push-button; the throb of the engines ceased as if by magic and the D-17 seemed to halt in her track.

Jack approached Lord Hastings.

"Mine, sir," he said, quietly.

CHAPTER II.

WITHIN THE FORTRESS.

"Good work, Jack," said Frank, approvingly.

"What do you advise?" asked Lord Hastings. "Up or down?"

"Depends on the depth, sir," replied Jack.

"We'll have a look at the chart," said Lord Hastings.

He spread it out before him and the three pored over it for several moments.

"Here you are, sir," said Frank, at last, placing a finger on the chart.

"Plenty of water," was Lord Hastings' comment. "Submerge another five fathoms, Mr. Templeton."

Jack gave the order and then returned to his post.

The D-17 submerged another five fathoms and proceeded at a snail's pace. Jack kept his eyes glued to the course ahead.

Half an hour later the vibrations of the engine ceased. Then Jack made his way aft to where Lord Hastings and Frank were conversing.

"Unless I am badly off in my calculations," said Lord Hastings, "we should now be able to come to the surface beyond the mine field."

"And as soon as we do, some German warship will send us to the bottom," remarked Frank dryly.

"So they will — if they see us," returned his commander. "We must make it a point that they do not see us. That's all."

"All very well, sir," said Jack, "but if we go up now they are sure to see us — and they won't mistake us for one of themselves this time."

Lord Hastings smiled quietly.

"Then we won't go up now," he replied as he looked at his watch and noted that it was half past five. "It'll be dark in less than an hour. We'll remain here until then."

This ended the conversation and the commander of the D-17 went to his cabin, leaving Jack in command.

The time passed slowly, but darkness came at last; and with its coming Lord Hastings emerged from his cabin, attired in the uniform of a German lieutenant-commander.

"I forgot to tell you lads to don your German uniforms," he said. "I'll wait now, but make haste."

Frank and Jack hurried away in response to this command and soon were attired in the full regalia of German lieutenants. Lord Hastings eyed them approvingly.

"There is no use talking," he said, "I have always thought it — and I am sure of it now — both of you would make first-class Germans. You may give the command to come to the surface, Mr. Templeton."

A few moments later the D-17 rode gently upon the calm sea within the fortifications of Heligoland, the greatest German military fortresses, and considered among the strongest and most impregnable in the world.

It was very dark and the night was perfectly still when the three forms ascended the ladder and emerged from the conning tower to the bridge — open now that the submarine was above water. A fourth figure followed them, that of Price, an aged British tar, whom Lord Hastings had designated to take command in their absence.

"Don't forget now, Price," said Lord Hastings sternly, "you will submerge immediately we have put off and on no account will you come to the surface again until 9 o'clock to-morrow night. Then you will rise in exactly this spot — and be sure that you are on time. Do I make myself clear?"

"Perfectly, sir," replied Price, saluting.

"Good. Then launch the boat."

This was done immediately and a few moments later Lord Hastings, Jack and Frank were proceeding rapidly shoreward, the engine of the small motor-boat muffled so that all that could be heard was the faint sound of the exhaust.

In the darkness, as they sped on, loomed great, dark shapes—the forms of some of the most powerful of the Kaiser's formidable sea fighters. Smoke poured from their funnels and faint lights glowed aboard.

"Ready for action at any moment," said Lord Hastings.

"So they are," agreed Frank. "Great Scott! It doesn't seem possible that so many of these great craft could be afraid to venture forth to give battle."

"No, it doesn't," declared Jack. "But at the same time, you must remember there are more and still more formidable craft waiting for them to come out and try it."

"That's true, too," admitted Frank. "I wish they would try it, though. I don't believe many of them would get back."

"Evidently the Germans have the same belief—which is the reason they haven't tried it," said Lord Hastings, smiling in the darkness.

"Silence, now," he cautioned them, after a moment. "We are close to the shore. Let all further talk be in German."

Five minutes later the motor-boat came to a long pier, which extended far into the water.

"Here we are," said Lord Hastings in German. He glanced around. "Other boats tied up here. Guess we might as well do the same," he said. "We may need it. Fortunately, at my suggestion, none of the D-17's boats bear a mark of identification. Guess it won't be bothered."

The three climbed up on the pier and the boat was made fast.

"Which way now, sir?" asked Frank.

"We'll just do a little prowling," said Lord Hastings.

He turned and was about to move off when there came a gruff hail:

"Who goes there?"

"Friend!" replied Lord Hastings, wheeling about quickly and looking into the heavy-joweled face of a German sentinel.

The German eyed the three figures keenly; then, apparently satisfied that they were all they seemed, he brought his hand up in a stiff military salute. The three passed on.

"Rather lax methods here, if you ask me," said Frank, when they were out of hearing.

"Oh, I don't know," said Jack. "You must remember that they feel perfectly secure. Evidently they have no idea an enemy would venture within this fortification."

"Some of them have ventured within ours," returned Frank.

"Just the egotism of the German, that's all," said Lord Hastings. "They all believe they can do things that no other man would even consider."

"So they do," declared Frank.

Jack looked at his chum in surprise.

"Just what do you mean by that?" he demanded.

"Oh, I was just thinking of the Lusitania, and a few other things."

"That's different," said Jack.

They continued their walk.

Now they came to a brilliantly lighted street.

"I didn't know this was a regular city," was Frank's comment.

"Neither is it," returned Lord Hastings, "although there are some few people living here."

"But look," protested Frank, pointing, "those are restaurants and cafés; and there are stores and things."

"So there are," returned his commander. "Must have changed since I was here last. However, I suppose it is because the garrison has to have some form of entertainment. Guess the best thing we can do is to go in one of these cafés and look about a bit."

He led the way, and just before entering the brilliantly lighted doorway, paused long enough to say in a low voice:

"No hesitation now. It would prove fatal. Walk as if you owned the place —
just as every German does."

The boys needed no instructions along this line, and they followed Lord
Hastings with heads erect, swaggering a trifle.

Inside there was revelry. German officers sat about tables that lined the
four walls of the room. With them, or some of them, were their wives.
Apparently it was the supper hour.

At a far end of the room a string orchestra furnished music and there were
four singers — two men and two women — or rather one young girl, for such
Frank perceived her to be after careful inspection.

A courteous waiter met the three at the door as they entered, and with
many bows ushered them to a table in a distant corner. They sat down and
Lord Hastings gave the order for supper.

Now the music struck up a more lively gait and some of the German
officers and their wives arose and danced in the center of the floor. Frank
saw a young German lieutenant, who apparently had been drinking,
approach the youthful singer. Apparently he asked her to dance, for he
indicated the other whirling couples. But the girl shook her head.
Whereupon the young German muttered something under his breath and
took himself away.

Frank found his eyes continually straying toward the young girl; and once
aware of his scrutiny, the girl's eyes also flashed in his direction more often
than was necessary. Jack noticed this, but said nothing.

But there was something else that Jack noticed as he ate. The young
German who had so recently been refused by the girl, had followed the
direction of her eyes and he now glared at Frank balefully. Jack smiled to
himself.

But the lad's smile soon changed to a frown.

After five minutes, the young German officer again approached the girl
and again asked her to dance. He met a second refusal and this time words

12

ensued. The German seemed angry and two of his companions approached and pulled him away.

Frank had been a witness of this scene, as had Jack and Lord Hastings.

"The big bully!" said Frank half aloud. "Just because he wears a German uniform he thinks he owns the earth. I would like to teach him a lesson."

"Don't try it here," said Lord Hastings quietly. "Remember where we are and the position we are in."

"Oh, I won't, sir," replied Frank. "But I don't like that fellow's looks."

"You don't, eh?" said Jack. "Well, how about the pretty singer. I notice you have been looking that way quite often."

Frank's face grew red.

"She doesn't look like a German to me," he said.

"No, she doesn't," Jack agreed. "Still, she must be or she wouldn't be here. Besides, she hasn't a trace of accent."

"Neither have you and you are not German," declared Frank.

Jack would have replied, but his attention was suddenly drawn again to the girl, who now seemed to be making signals to catch Frank's eye.

"Seems to want to talk to you," said Jack, nudging his chum slyly.

At that moment the girl looked directly at Frank and smiled. Then she motioned him to come to her. Frank was greatly flustered. Not so Jack.

"You'd better go. She probably wants you to dance with her," said Jack.

"Yes, you had better go, Frank," said Lord Hastings. "In the first place it would be impolite to refuse, and besides, it might attract attention. Only be careful."

Frank, his face still red, hesitated a moment; then rose to his feet.

CHAPTER III.

A WARNING.

Now, Frank, attired in his German uniform, made a handsome picture of a young officer and many eyes were turned his way as he strode across the floor. Particularly did the young German officer with whom the singer had refused to dance eye him, but his was not a gaze of admiration—it was anger.

Lord Hastings called Jack's attention to this.

"Oh, I've noticed it," said Jack. "I'll keep an eye on him. Now I wonder what that girl wants with Frank?"

Lord Hastings shrugged his shoulders.

"You have as much an idea as I have," was his reply.

The girl arose from her seat as Frank approached. She extended a hand, and, with the air of a true cavalier, Frank bent low over it. Then, as the music struck up, the girl smiled and would have spoken, but Frank forestalled her.

"Will you dance?" he asked.

She nodded; and a moment later they were whirling about the floor in an old-fashioned waltz.

Thus among the crowd there was a certain privacy and Frank was moved to ask:

"And now will you not tell me why you signalled me?"

Instantly the girl became serious, although she continued to smile.

"I must be brief," she said, "so listen closely. In the first place you are not German. Oh, I knew it the moment you came in," she said hurriedly, as Frank gave a start. "I wouldn't have mentioned it, but the young German officer whom I refused to dance with also suspects. He said as much when he noticed me looking at you. He said he would catch you off your guard and force you to betray yourself."

"But— —" Frank started to protest.

14

"Oh, there is no use trying to fool me," said the girl. "I know you are not a German—an Englishman perhaps, eh?"

Frank smiled at her.

"No; not an Englishman," he replied.

"You are not French," said the girl, looking up at him. "Even though you speak German without accent, I know you are not French, for I myself am French and I would detect it."

"No; I am not French," said Frank with another smile.

"Then what?" asked the girl.

"Well," said Frank, "what would you say to an American."

"An American!" exclaimed the girl. "Are you, really? I am glad, for I have wanted to meet an American."

Suddenly Frank gave another start.

"Great Scott!" he thought. "Suppose this girl is fooling me? Suppose she has taken this means of finding out who we are?"

He looked at her suspiciously. But the girl evidently read his thoughts, for she looked at him steadily and said:

"No, I will not betray you. You need have no fear."

"But if you are French," said Frank, "what are you doing here?"

"It's a long story," said the girl, "and some day I may tell you. But now I have not time. The music will stop in a moment or two now, and you must return to your friends. But I had to warn you, for I know that Lieutenant Holzen is bent on mischief. It would be well for you and your friends to leave at once."

"Thanks," said Frank, "but we are able to take care of ourselves."

"Oh, I know that," responded the girl. "But I know also that you would not be here except upon some desperate mission and that you cannot afford to jeopardize for the sake of a quarrel."

"You are right, of course," said Frank quietly. "But tell me, what is my mission to you?"

"Nothing," said the girl slowly, "only that—that I would do anything for France."

She said it gravely and there could be no mistaking her earnestness. Frank bowed his head in reply; for there was nothing he could say.

Several times more they whirled about the room; and then Frank bethought himself to ask the girl who she was.

"Will you tell me your name?" he asked. "I am Lieutenant Chadwick of His British Majesty's service."

The girl smiled and would have replied, but at that moment the music ceased. Frank offered her his arm and led her back to her seat and there was no further opportunity for the girl to reply to the lad's last question. As she resumed her seat, Frank bowed once more, then turned on his heel and strode back to his own table, where Lord Hastings and Jack were awaiting him eagerly.

"Well, fair charmer," Jack greeted him. "How — —"

Frank silenced his chum with a gesture.

"This is a serious business," he said quietly and told the others what the girl had said.

"And you admitted it?" exclaimed Jack in a subdued voice. "She'll tell every German in forty miles."

"No, she won't," declared Frank. "She was telling the truth."

Jack laughed aloud.

"Of all the credulous — —" he began.

"Look here. I tell you she was telling the truth," declared Frank angrily.

Again Jack laughed and Frank was about to make another angry remark when Lord Hastings interfered.

"Perhaps Frank is right," he said quietly. "At all events, it is nothing for you two to fight about."

"We're not fighting, sir," said Jack. "But the idea — —"

"The idea nothing!" Frank broke in. "I guess I know what I am talking about. I danced with her, didn't I? You didn't."

"Ha! ha!" said Jack. "You see, sir, he brags about it. She's fooled him, all right."

"Don't you believe it, sir," declared Frank. "I tell you, sir, the girl was telling me the truth. Why, sir, you have only to look at her — —"

"Now we have it, sir," exclaimed Jack. "That's it. You have only to look at her. Ha! ha!"

"I tell you — —" Frank began angrily again.

Jack made his chum a bow across the table.

"You are right," he said with a superior air that only angered Frank the more. "She told you the truth."

"Enough of this," interposed Lord Hastings. "No matter whether she told the truth or not, we are in danger. If she didn't tell the truth we are likely to be set upon at any moment and if she did the German officer probably will make trouble. The best thing we can do is get out of here."

He signaled the waiter and paid the check.

"Come," he said and got to his feet.

The waiter brought their hats and cloaks and Lord Hastings moved toward the door. Jack followed him and Frank came last.

On the way to the door it was necessary to pass the table at which the German officer and his companions were seated. Lord Hastings walked by without a glance, as did Jack. Frank would have followed, but the German suddenly jumped to his feet and confronted him with an imprecation.

"Stand aside," said Frank quietly.

The German made no move to comply. At first Frank thought of pushing the man away; then changed his mind, for he realized that such an act would draw all eyes to them. The best plan was to get by quietly if possible.

"What is it?" he asked.

"It is my belief that you are a spy," declared the German.

"Yes?" said Frank inquiringly. "Well, sir, every man has a right to his own opinion; you as well as another."

"Smart, aren't you?" sneered the German. He raised his hand suddenly and, before Frank could realize his intention, slapped the lad smartly across the face.

Frank took a step forward and his hands clenched. His face turned red and he was about to return the blow. A second time his better judgment prevailed and he stepped back, remarking quietly:

"You shall answer for that, Lieutenant Holzen!"

"What! you know my name?" exclaimed the German. "So I shall answer, eh? Yes, so I shall, at any time and place that suits your convenience."

"I am no duelist," said Frank quietly.

"No; you are a coward," was the retort.

Again Frank's face turned red and his hands clenched; but he restrained himself.

"For that you shall answer also," he said. "Now, stand aside. I would pass."

"Not much!" said Lieutenant Holzen. "First you must tell me the time and place of meeting."

"Look here, I'm getting tired of this foolishness," said Frank. "Get out of my way."

"What do you mean by speaking like that to me?" demanded the German angrily. "You shall pass when I allow you to pass, not before."

"If you don't get out of my way immediately, I shall have to throw you out," said Frank very quietly, which was a sure sign that his anger was reaching the bursting point.

"So?" said the German with a laugh. "Now, I say — —"

"You've said enough," cried Frank suddenly.

He struck out suddenly with his right fist. The blow went true. Struck upon the point of the jaw, the German reeled back. Frank straightened him up again with a left-handed hook to the stomach and then sent his right fist to the jaw a second time. The German officer sprawled across the table.

Before any of the others could interfere Frank dashed toward the door where Lord Hastings and Jack stood, having watched developments with the assurance that Frank could take care of himself.

All dashed out together.

"This way!" cried Lord Hastings.

The others followed close on his heels.

Behind, as they darted round a corner, they could hear the hue and cry of the pursuers.

"We'll have to do some sprinting," declared Lord Hastings.

For perhaps fifteen minutes they ran, turning corner after corner, and at last, when Lord Hastings felt they were safe from pursuit, he drew up for a much needed breath.

"Can't tell whether they'll follow us or not," he said. "If they take any stock in the officer's story that we are spies, they will. If they think it is just a private quarrel, the chances are they won't. However, we can do no particular good here. We'll have to go back and see."

"Anything you say, sir," agreed Frank. "I suppose I shouldn't have hit that fellow, but he wouldn't let me by."

"Don't worry about that. You did exactly right," declared Lord Hastings. "Come on."

He led the way in the direction from which they had come.

CHAPTER IV.

MARIE DULCÉ.

Things seemed to have quieted down when the three found themselves again before the café. Apparently there had been but a faint-hearted pursuit. All breathed easier.

"They can't have believed very much in that spy story," remarked Frank.

"It would seem that way," agreed Lord Hastings. "Evidently they took your friend's words as the ravings of a man intoxicated."

"A good thing, too, sir," said Jack. "None of them will molest us, unless it is the doughty lieutenant himself."

"We don't need to worry about him, I guess," said Lord Hastings. "Now we must get busy. I wonder — —" as a sudden thought struck him, "if your friend," he turned to Frank, "the young lady, I mean, couldn't give us, or get for us, the information we desire."

"I guess she could, sir," replied Frank, "if we could find her."

"She probably is still in the café," said Jack.

"And so probably is Lieutenant Holzen," replied Frank dryly.

"True," said Lord Hastings. "We can't afford to risk another encounter. Guess we'll have to hunt up the place she lives. All we have to do is ask where Mademoiselle — by the way, Frank, what is her name?"

"I don't know, sir. She didn't tell me."

"What?" exclaimed Lord Hastings in surprise. "You are a nice gallant, you are. So you failed to find out her name, eh?"

"Yes, sir. She was just going to tell me when the music stopped."

Jack laughed.

"Maybe she wasn't so anxious to tell you," he said.

"Now look here," said Frank, "don't let's start that again. If it touches you on a sore spot, I'll drop the subject."

"Oh, all right," said Jack.

"Well, the matter should not be so difficult, anyhow," declared Lord Hastings. "We'll ask someone the name of the young lady who sings."

"Perfectly simple, sir," agreed Jack. "Whom shall we ask?"

"The first person we see," was the reply.

Lord Hastings led the way down the street. An officer approached. Lord Hastings accosted him in German.

"I have recently been ordered to Heligoland," he said. "A moment ago I was in yonder café," pointing, "and the young singer in there bears such a striking resemblance to the daughter of a friend of mine that I should like to know if she is the same."

"And the name of the young lady to whom you refer?" questioned the German.

"Henrietta! Henrietta Blucher!"

The German laughed.

"Then you are mistaken," he said pleasantly. "The young lady who sings in yonder café is Marie Dulcé and she is a French girl."

"I had not taken her to be French," returned Lord Hastings. "Can you tell me where she lives?"

"Why, certainly," was the reply, and the German named an address and gave the necessary directions for getting there. "I don't imagine," he added, "you will find her home much before 12 o'clock, the café does not close until eleven."

Lord Hastings thanked the man and the latter took himself off.

"Well, we have that much to go on, anyhow," said Lord Hastings. "Now the best thing for us to do is to go to Mlle. Dulcé's home and await her arrival."

"And maybe they won't let us in," said Jack.

"We'll have to chance that."

An hour later they sought the address given and mounted the steps. Lord Hastings rang the bell. A pleasant-appearing woman of middle age answered their summons. At a glance Lord Hastings knew she was French and he addressed her in that language.

"Could it be that you are Madame Dulcé?" he inquired courteously.

The woman smiled as she answered in the affirmative.

"We," said Lord Hastings, indicating Frank and Jack as well as himself, "would have a few words with your daughter Marie when she returns home. We have sought her here rather than at the café for several reasons."

A look of deep anxiety spread itself over Madame Dulcé's face and she asked excitedly:

"What has she done, sir? Surely she will not be arrested? You do not take her for a spy?"

"You need have no fear," returned Lord Hastings reassuringly. "We mean no harm. May we come in and wait?"

"Certainly."

Madame Dulcé led the way into a small, though cozy parlor and took their hats and coats.

"Marie will be here soon after twelve," she said. "She always comes straight home, for she knows I worry about her."

"How does it happen that she sings in the café?" asked Lord Hastings.

"Because we are so poor," was the reply. "Her salary there enables us to keep the wolf away from the door. Frau Heffler, who also sings, was the one who so kindly gave her the opportunity."

"I see," said Lord Hastings, and became silent.

The time passed slowly; but it passed. Frank waited eagerly, for he was anxious to see the girl again. Jack noticed the look on his chum's face and remarked:

"Now just be patient. Marie will soon be here."

Frank smiled.

"It's not as bad as that, I assure you," he returned.

Came the sound of light footsteps without. A key turned in the front door and the footsteps came toward the parlor.

"You have company, mother?" asked the girl's voice as she tripped forward.

"Some gentlemen to see you, Marie," was the reply.

In the doorway the girl stood spellbound for a brief instant, as she made out the faces of the callers. At first she did not recognize Lord Hastings and Jack, but she knew Frank instantly.

"Lieutenant Chadwick!" she exclaimed.

She came forward with outstretched hand and again Frank bent low over it.

"But tell me," she said. "How were you able to find my home? And what is it you want of me?"

"I found your home by asking," returned Frank. "As for what we want, I would first present my commander and brother officer to you."

Introductions followed all around and then the girl repeated her question.

"I would rather," said Lord Hastings, giving Marie a sharp look, "if we could speak with you alone."

"But my mother — —" protested the girl.

"I know," continued Lord Hastings, "but she need have no fear."

Madame Dulcé arose and smiled.

"I shall leave you," she said. "When you have finished your talk, will you call me, Marie?"

The girl nodded and Madame Dulcé left the room.

"Now, gentlemen," said Marie, turning to the others.

"As commander of this party," said Lord Hastings with a smile, "I guess it is up to me, as the Americans say, to do the talking." He gazed at the girl earnestly. "You know something of us already," he added, "so there is no harm in putting ourselves further in your power."

"You need have no fear that I shall betray you," said the girl.

"I had no such thought," responded Lord Hastings courteously. "Well, then the situation is this," and he told her why they had come to Heligoland.

"And what is it you want of me?" said the girl, when he had concluded.

"Recalling what you told Mr. Chadwick you would do for France," said Lord Hastings quietly, "I am here to put you to the test."

The girl sprang to her feet and her eyes flashed for a brief instant. Then she sat down again.

"Try me," she said quietly.

Lord Hastings nodded his satisfaction.

"Then," said he, "can you tell me something of the fortifications of Heligoland? Can you tell me its weak spots and its strong? Can you tell me how many men there are here — how many battleships? In short, can you tell me anything that will be of value to the Allies?"

"I can," was the quiet reply. "Ever since the war broke out I have been learning things — and trying to learn more — and I have stored them up in my memory for just this chance. It has been my ambition to serve France and it makes me happy to think I can do so at last."

"Good," said Lord Hastings. "Then perhaps the best way will be for you to answer my questions."

"Bien, Lord Hastings."

"First, then, from what you have learned, where is the weakest spot in the fortifications — the spot that would be most susceptible to attack?"

"I can answer that quickly," was the reply. "There is none."

"The number of ships in the harbor?" was Lord Hastings' next question.

"At the moment, seventy-two, cruisers, dreadnoughts and torpedo boats. The others are in the Kiel Canal, or in the Baltic."

"And the number of men now stationed here?"

"I can't answer that exactly, but the number is comparatively small. I can find out in the morning."

"We'll pass that for the moment, then. Is there a submarine base here, or do the underwater boats operate from Kiel?"

"There is a submarine base here."

Thus Lord Hastings questioned the girl at length and she answered quietly and comprehensively. The conversation continued for more than an hour. Lord Hastings, Jack and Frank storing what the girl told them in their memories for future use.

"And now," said Lord Hastings, "for the final question."

Marie Dulcé smiled.

"I'm ready," she said.

"Is there any way in which you can procure for me a map of the fortress itself, including all its details?"

For a brief moment the girl was silent. Then she sprang to her feet, her eyes once again flashing.

"I can and I will!" she cried determinedly. "You shall have the paper to-morrow night before eight o'clock."

CHAPTER V.

THAT NIGHT.

The conversation having come to this point, Lord Hastings considered further words useless. He was deeply impressed by the bearing of the young French girl and he had no doubt that she would do what she said — or, at least, that it would not be her fault if she failed; nor, for that matter, had Frank or Jack.

"Well," said Lord Hastings after a short silence, "that settles that, then. I don't suppose you will tell me your plan?"

The girl shook her head and smiled.

"It's hardly necessary," she replied. "Now, if you wish, I shall have mother make a place here for you for the night. I don't suppose you have any other place to go?"

Lord Hastings shook his head negatively, and half an hour later the three found themselves in a cozy little room on the second floor, in which there were two beds.

"You may sleep securely here," was Madame Dulcé's parting words.

Neither Jack, Frank, nor the commander wasted much time getting into bed, for they were all tired out and a few moments later they were asleep.

All were astir early in the Dulcé home the following morning, in spite of the lateness of the hour at which they had retired.

"I suppose you will be on your mission this morning?" asked Lord Hastings of Marie.

"No," replied the girl with a smile. "To-night will be time enough. I shall spend the day here entertaining you."

Lord Hastings made a gallant response, but he did not press the girl for the method she intended to pursue.

The day passed pleasantly and swiftly. Night came only too soon, thought Frank, who was beginning to admire the young French girl immensely.

Dusk fell soon after five o'clock and Marie made ready to go. Heavily cloaked and muffled, she turned in the door as she was about to leave.

"If you will venture to the café again to-night," she said, "I shall have the papers for you. There is no other place where I can give them to you, so you will have to risk another visit."

"We shall be there," said Frank. "I guess we can avoid Lieutenant Holzen some way, if he should be there."

"He is always there," replied Marie and a moment later she was gone.

"I guess we had better wait a while," said Lord Hastings. "Nothing was ever gained by being in a rush."

Accordingly it was an hour later—almost half-past six o'clock—when the three came again to the little café.

Lord Hastings entered jauntily, not the slightest nervousness in his manner, though his right hand in the pocket of his great coat rested upon the butt of his revolver. Frank and Jack, close behind, also had a hand thrust into their pockets and there was no need to mention what lay within the palm of each.

A waiter approached and conducted them to a table at the far end of the room, but one removed from the one they had had the night before. Lord Hastings gave the order and then, for the first time, glanced around.

There was no sign of Lieutenant Holzen.

Across the room Marie was preparing to sing and a hush fell over the diners,—which continued until she had finished. Following came a roar of approval. It was while she was responding to an encore that Lieutenant Holzen entered.

Frank was the first to see him and gave a start. He spoke to Lord Hastings in a whisper.

"Keep your nerve, now," was his commander's quiet response. "If he comes over here, let me deal with him."

Frank said nothing.

Now Marie had resumed her seat. Lieutenant Holzen, after glancing toward her, swept the room with his eyes. As he perceived Lord Hastings and his two officers, he clenched his hands and took a step forward.

For a moment Frank could see that he was plainly undecided just what to do; then the German hastily approached.

Frank gripped the table with both hands.

Before the three, Lieutenant Holzen paused. His eyes rested upon Frank.

"Last night," he said, "when I was somewhat the worse for wear, you struck me. I demand either an apology or the satisfaction due from one gentleman to another."

Lord Hastings answered for Frank.

"If my friend here has insulted you," he said quietly, "it is but right that you should demand an accounting. We shall be here all evening. If you will send a friend to me, we shall arrange the details."

The German bowed and Lord Hastings, Frank and Jack did likewise. Then turning on his heel, Lieutenant Holzen walked away.

Frank kept an eye on him and saw that the young German spent most of his time gazing at Marie. Looking in her direction, he was surprised to see the girl return the young officer's smile. She nodded to him.

Frank mentioned the matter to Lord Hastings, and added:

"I don't like it."

"Ho! Ho!" laughed Jack. "So you are getting jealous, eh?"

Frank flushed.

"You know better than that," he replied sharply. "I just don't like it; that's all."

Suddenly, in response to a smile from Marie, Lieutenant Holzen arose and approached her. The music was about to commence and Frank realized what was going to happen. For some reason he could not explain to himself he felt decidedly uncomfortable and shifted uneasily in his seat.

Jack noticed this and was about to make a remark greatly to his chum's discomfort, when Lord Hastings stayed him with a gesture.

"Quiet now," he said, "and if I am not mistaken and you look sharp, you may see something interesting."

The music struck up at this juncture and Marie and Lieutenant Holzen glided smoothly across the floor. Lord Hastings, Jack and Frank followed them with their eyes.

At last the music stopped. The young German escorted Marie back to her place and returned to his own table.

Time passed swiftly now for the three British officers. Again Marie danced with the young German officer, and yet a third time. But when he came for his fourth dance, she shook her head and inclined it toward Frank.

The latter had been watching her eagerly and this time he did not hesitate. Getting quickly to his feet he strode across the room and offered the girl his arm. A moment later the music struck up again and the two glided across the floor much to the discomfiture of the young German, who stood gnawing his mustache and fingering his sword belt.

Suddenly Frank felt the girl's hand slide into his inside breast pocket and heard the faint crumple of paper. He was about to speak, but Marie silenced him with a warning: "Sh-h-h."

Half a moment later she whispered:

"The papers you are after are in your pocket. I took them from Lieutenant Holzen as we danced."

Frank made no reply, but he pressed slightly the fingers that rested so lightly in his own. It was a signal and the girl understood.

"Now go immediately," she whispered, as the music came to a stop and Frank led her back to her place.

But first Frank must needs lean over her hand again to say good-bye.

"I shall see you again, some time," he said.

Marie smiled, but said nothing. Frank returned to the others.

"I have the papers," he said quietly to Lord Hastings.

"Good! I had surmised as much," was his commander's reply.

"She said that we had better go immediately," said Frank.

"We can't do that," said Lord Hastings. "You may remember we have an appointment with a friend of Lieutenant Holzen."

It was half an hour later that this friend approached them. Lord Hastings rose to greet him, as did Jack. Frank remained seated.

The newcomer introduced himself and Lord Hastings gave a fictitious name, also introducing Jack and Frank in the same manner. Then they went into details of the duel.

"As the challenged party," said Lord Hastings, thinking to keep up appearances, "we have the choice of weapons." The German bowed. "Then," said Lord Hastings, "we name revolvers at twenty paces."

"Good. And the time?"

Lord Hastings seemed to consider for a moment. At last he said:

"In the morning at six o'clock."

"And the place?"

"That shall rest with you."

The man designated a spot and Lord Hastings announced that it would be satisfactory. The German bowed and took his departure.

"Nothing like keeping up appearances, sir," said Jack with a smile. "To have heard you talk, no one would have expected that you knew the duel was not coming off."

"I flatter myself it wasn't done so badly," returned Lord Hastings modestly.

"And how soon shall we go, sir?" asked Frank. Lord Hastings produced his watch.

"Eight o'clock," he said, putting the timepiece back in his pocket. "We haven't much time, and yet we have considerable. I believe we had as well stay here until half-past. We can make it in that time."

"As you will, sir," returned Frank, and settled back in his chair to enjoy the music.

But his enjoyment of the music was to be short-lived. Trouble came suddenly and unexpectedly.

Frank, chancing to glance toward Lieutenant Holzen, saw that worthy put his hand to his breast pocket. Immediately his face turned red and he sprang to his feet. Hurriedly he thrust his hands into all his pockets. Then his face turned from red to white.

Frank nudged Lord Hastings.

"Holzen has discovered his loss, sir," he said quietly. "Had we better move?"

Lord Hastings sat still.

"Too bad," he said calmly. "I am afraid this means trouble. We'll probably have to fight and run. Guns ready, boys."

The lads dropped both hands to the holsters that hung on either side of their belts. They were ready.

"We'll let him start the trouble," said Lord Hastings quietly. "Then we'll make a break for the door."

Lieutenant Holzen was not long starting the trouble. He sprang to his feet with a shout.

"There are traitors and spies in this room!" he shouted.

CHAPTER VI.

FLIGHT.

Frank made a move to rise. Lord Hastings stayed him.

"Wait!" was all he said.

Immediately following Lieutenant Holzen's words, there was a terrible commotion in the café. Officers jumped quickly to their feet. Several rushed to Lieutenant Holzen, who still stood there gesticulating wildly.

"Traitors! Spies!" he cried.

"Be calm," said one of the officers. "Tell me what is the matter?"

"My papers!" shouted the young German. "My papers! The charts of the fortress! They are gone."

"Impossible!" cried one of the others. "You must be mistaken. Look through your pockets again."

"I looked through them!" was the shouted response. "See here! and here!" and he turned them all wrong side out.

"Perhaps you left them in your rooms," said another officer.

"No. I brought them with me. I had them when I sat down."

"But no one has come near you," said one of his companions. "But wait a moment. You danced with Mlle. Dulcé. Could she have taken them? You danced with her several times; yet, on previous nights, I have noticed that she avoided you. It must be she."

"Yes! It must be she!" cried Lieutenant Holzen. "Arrest her!"

Half-a-dozen men moved down the room toward where Marie Dulcé stood smiling. It was at that moment that Lord Hastings gave the signal to rise.

"Up and run for the door!" he cried. "Shoot the first man who draws a gun!"

He suited the action to the word, and the two lads were right behind him.

Before Lord Hastings loomed up the figure of a German colonel. The commander of the D-17 fired point-blank and the man fell to the floor. Lord Hastings dashed on.

Now Marie took a hand in things herself. As one of the Germans would have seized her, she stepped quickly backward and reached upward on the wall. There her hand found what she knew it would find — an electric switch. Quickly she threw it and the room was plunged into utter darkness.

Eluding the grasp of the man who reached for her in the darkness, Marie stepped quickly forward. Keeping close to the wall, she made her way toward the front door. On all sides men shouted and women screamed, but the girl went on calmly.

Occasional revolver flashes lighted up the darkness, but only momentarily.

Lord Hastings, reaching the door, found it barred by two men. Before he could bring his revolver to bear, an outstretched arm sent it spinning from his hand. Lord Hastings growled and struck out with his fist. An arm encircled his neck and held him powerless. At the same time a voice called out:

"I've got one of them!"

Jack, who was immediately behind his commander, although he could not see what was going on, realized from the German's words what was up, and called out:

"Where are you, sir?"

"Here," came the reply. "A man has me around the neck."

Jack's lips shut grimly, and, leaving Frank to guard their rear, he stepped quickly forward and laid his hand on a man's arm.

"Have I hold of you, or the enemy, sir?" he asked quietly.

"Must be the German," was the reply.

Jack ran his hand up the arm until he felt a face. Then he drew back his left arm and his fist crashed forward.

"All right," said Lord Hastings. "You've dropped him."

33

The second man who had blocked the doorway now closed in, but Jack disposed of him quickly. Shots came from behind, and Frank's voice cried:

"Getting too warm, sir. Let's move."

"Come on, then," said Jack.

He threw his weight against the door, and it crashed open. A moment later all three were in the street and running in the direction of the water.

A crowd of Germans poured from the café after them, and the crack of revolvers sounded like a rapid-fire gun in action.

"We'll have to hurry!" cried Lord Hastings. "They'll have the whole fortress on our heels in a moment."

Directly the water front came into view.

"Here we are!" cried Lord Hastings. "Quick, now!"

He made directly toward the D-17's motorboat, which he could see was where he had left it, but at that moment a figure blocked the way. It was a German sentinel, and his rifle was pointed squarely at Lord Hastings.

"Halt!" he said sternly.

Lord Hastings stopped in his tracks.

"What's all the row back there?" demanded the sentry.

Lord Hastings would have replied, but Jack did not give him time.

Stepping suddenly from behind Lord Hastings, he dived at the German's legs. He had gauged the distance accurately, and the two went to the ground violently. The sentry's gun was discharged, but the bullet whistled harmlessly over Lord Hastings's head.

"No time to fool with him, Jack!" cried Lord Hastings. "Here come the others. Hurry!"

Jack raised his opponent's head in his two hands, then bumped it against the ground.

"There," he said, rising, "that'll keep him for a while."

He hurried after the others, who had jumped into the boat.

"Cut the line there—quick!" commanded Lord Hastings.

Frank obeyed just as Jack tumbled aboard.

"All right, sir. All here," said the latter.

"Good," said Lord Hastings.

The boat moved off, slowly at first, then faster and faster.

By the time the German pursuers had reached the water's edge, the boat was beyond revolver shot, though still within range of rifles.

"Down!" cried Lord Hastings, as a bullet whistled overhead.

The others obeyed.

"They'll be after us, sir!" shouted Frank.

"They'll have to hurry if they want to catch us," declared Lord Hastings.

"Say! What time is it?" asked Frank suddenly.

"Why?" demanded his chum.

"Why," repeated Frank, "because if we get out here before nine o'clock we might just as well stay ashore. Price will not come to the surface until nine sharp."

By the flare of a match he struck, Jack gazed at his watch.

"No need to worry there, then," he said. "It's three minutes to nine right now."

"Pretty lucky," said Frank.

"Rather," commented Lord Hastings dryly. "Look back and see if they are following us."

"Yes, sir, twenty of them," replied Frank, after a glance over his shoulder.

"Well, we'll have time, unless they are armed with cannon," said Lord Hastings. "All we need is to get aboard the D-17. Rifle shots won't hurt us then."

Rifle bullets continued to fly over and about the motorboat, one occasionally striking home. But none of the occupants was touched.

"We must be about the place," said Frank suddenly.

"About a minute more," responded Lord Hastings.

The minute up, Lord Hastings shut off the engine. They gazed about.

"If Price doesn't come up pretty quick, we'll have to run for it," said the commander quietly. "It's time now."

"He'll be up unless something has gone wrong," said Jack positively.

"Unless he's gone to sleep," declared Frank.

"Well, I wish he'd hurry," said Jack. "We can't remain here many minutes longer. They are getting too close."

"So they are," agreed Lord Hastings. "We'll wait thirty seconds, then, if there is not some sign of the D-17, we'll move. We'll make a fight for it, at any rate."

The seconds ticked off slowly; and then, just as Lord Hastings was ready to open the engine, the waters of the sea parted and the neat outline of the D-17 appeared upon the surface.

A moment later the conning tower opened and Price stepped on deck. The submarine was perhaps fifty yards away, and Lord Hastings ran the motorboat toward it at full speed.

"Here we are, Price!" he called.

"All right, sir?"

"All right, but pursued. Below with you, and be ready to submerge the minute we are below."

"Aye, aye, sir!"

Price disappeared.

A moment later the motorboat scraped alongside the submarine, and the three clambered over the side as fast as they could amid a veritable rain of bullets, none of which, however, found its mark.

"Down with you, quick!" shouted Lord Hastings.

Frank and Jack dashed for the companionway at top speed, Lord Hastings right behind them. Down the ladder they went with a rush, and the conning tower was hermetically closed behind them.

"Submerge to ten fathoms, and quickly, Mr. Templeton!" said Lord Hastings quietly.

Jack repeated the command, slowly the tanks began to fill, and the D-17 to submerge, the while the occupants of the motorboats without peppered the side of the vessel with rifle and revolver bullets.

"Shall I launch a torpedo at them, sir?" asked Frank.

Lord Hastings shook his head.

"Not much use," he said. "You might hit one, and you might not. It's not worth a chance. But we haven't any time to lose now. They know we're here, and the quicker we get out the better. They'll have every German submarine in these waters on the hunt for us. Fortunately, we have the heels of any of them, and we can still see while submerged. They don't know that; so, for the moment, the advantage is on our side."

"But, sir," protested Jack, "how about the other part of our plans here?"

"What?" demanded Lord Hastings.

"Warship, or two, sir," said Jack.

"True," said Lord Hastings. "I had forgotten. Shape your course due north for two miles, Mr. Templeton; then come to the surface."

He turned to Frank and spoke again:

"We'll leave our card, at any rate," he said quietly. "You may prepare for action, Mr. Chadwick!"

CHAPTER VII.

THE ATTACK.

An instant later every man aboard the D-17 was on the alert. Lord Hastings stood at the periscope, which, immediately the submarine had reached the desired place, would make visible to him the great German battleships upon the surface of the water.

Frank and Jack stood to their posts, ready and eager for the word that would send one of the steel engines of destruction speeding into the hull of the enemy.

There was not a man aboard who did not realize that they were indeed in a ticklish situation; for, besides the danger that always attended such an undertaking, there was the additional danger now of encountering one or more of the German under-water boats.

Nor was there a chance of a surprise attack. Lord Hastings was well aware that the presence of a hostile submarine had been flashed to every German battleship in the harbor.

Above, the sea was being swept with powerful searchlights, while below the under-sea craft of the Germans were dashing hither and thither in a vain endeavor to find some trace of the enemy who had so brazenly dared to enter what the Germans believed an impenetrable base.

Lord Hastings now turned to Jack with a command:

"You may come to the surface, Mr. Templeton."

Jack repeated the command with alacrity; and when the D-17 had risen so that her periscope barely protruded above the top of the water, she was kept stationary.

"What do you see, sir?" asked Frank of Lord Hastings, who now peered intently into the periscope.

"German battleship half a mile to port and another half a mile astern," was the reply. "The others are too far away for us, although they might reach us with a shell if their lights should happen to pick us up. We'll make for the fellow to port and trust to luck that we get near enough without being spotted."

He gave the necessary directions to Frank, who had taken the wheel.

Fortune was with the D-17 this night, for the submarine approached within less than a hundred and fifty yards of the German battleship without being perceived. There, at a command from Lord Hastings, she became stationary.

"No. 1 torpedo!" commanded Lord Hastings suddenly, and gave the range.

Jack touched a little button, and the signal board flashed red.

"Attention!" was the next command that glowed in letters of fire.

The British sailor at No. 1 torpedo stood ready to release his instrument of destruction.

There was a slight pause. Then:

"Fire!"

Followed a slight metallic click as the engine of death sped on its way over the water.

Contrary to the expectations of the others, Lord Hastings did not immediately give the command to submerge. Instead, he stood perfectly motionless, peering into the periscope. There was silence aboard the D-17, broken finally by Frank, who could stand the suspense no longer:

"Did we hit her, sir?"

For answer, Lord Hastings stepped aside and motioned the lad to his place at the periscope. Frank, turning the wheel over to a sailor, sprang forward quickly. And here is what he saw:

A short distance to port, a huge German battleship was slowly sinking by the head. Fully half a hundred great searchlights — the eyes of the many other German ships of war — played upon the sinking vessel now, lighting her up like day. Movements aboard the sinking vessel were plainly visible to Frank.

Men rushed hither and thither in the greatest confusion, and while Frank could hear no sounds there below the water, there was every indication of shouts and cries of panic and of fright.

An officer rushed aft and sought to maintain some semblance of order among the members of the crew who were seeking to get a small boat over the side at that end of the ship. A German sailor struck him down with a blow of his fist and returned to his place at the boat.

Men struggled frantically. The German officer picked himself up and drew a revolver; then advanced again upon the sailors. One sprang forward, but fell sprawling upon the deck. No sound came to Frank, but he knew that the German officer had fired.

One, two, three others of the struggling sailors now fell before the revolver of the infuriated German officer; the others gave back. Frank saw the man gesticulating angrily; and the sailors fell to getting the boat over in a more orderly manner, apparently more afraid of the officer who confronted them with leveled revolver than they were of the imminent danger of the ship going to the bottom.

Forward, aboard the German battleship also were signs of confusion. There, too, officers had their hands full in attempting to maintain discipline. Several times one of their number fired into the faces of the crowd of sailors.

Suddenly the great German ship staggered visibly and a dull roar carried to the ears of those aboard the D-17.

"Explosion," Frank explained to those behind him.

"Fire aboard must have reached her magazine," said Lord Hastings.

And indeed such was the case. When the great ship staggered there was a terrible roar, louder than the loudest peal of thunder. Ensued a greater panic than before aboard the German vessel.

No longer did men fight for the boats. No longer did they heed the cries of their officers to stick to the ship and die like true German sailors. Instead, they rushed for the rails and threw themselves into the sea in scores.

Several times officers rushed in between them, but they were hurled aside. It was every man for himself now, and finally the officers gave up the attempt to check the panic.

As the sailors continued to leap into the sea, the officers congregated on the bridge, gathering about a tall figure, apparently the German commander.

And at length, besides these officers, there was not a man to be seen aboard the battleship. Then the commander raised his hand in a commanding gesture. A dozen of the score of officers left him and threw themselves into the sea after the sailors.

Another command from the German captain and others left his side, though plainly more reluctantly. This continued until, besides the commander, there were but two men left.

"His first officers, I suppose," Frank muttered to himself.

Again the German commander gesticulated angrily. The others argued back. The commander stamped his foot. One of the officers laid a hand on his arm. The commander shook it off.

"They want him to go along," said Frank, who had already explained the situation to Lord Hastings and the others within hearing.

"They are wasting time," said Lord Hastings. "I know these German naval commanders."

Frank peered across the water again.

Now both of the officers had hold of the commander and were seeking to drag him toward the side of the ship. Apparently they held him firmly, for Frank could see that he was trying hard to shake off their hands. But he was held too securely.

Even from where he stood, Frank could see the commander shrug his shoulders. Immediately the other officers released their hold. All moved toward the side.

"You're wrong this time, sir," said Frank to Lord Hastings. "The commander is going."

"I don't believe it," was the reply.

"Well, he is, sir. He — — "

Frank broke off suddenly, for there were new developments aboard the sinking battleship.

At the very side of the ship the commander hung back. The other officers protested. The captain was adamant. Again the others sought to seize him by the arms. But the commander had anticipated this action, and he leaped lightly backward, at the same time presenting a brace of revolvers. The others halted in their tracks.

Now the commander motioned the others over the side, gesticulating with his weapons. The others shook their heads. The commander raised both revolvers and pointed each at one of his officers. Still they shook their heads.

"By Jove!" said Frank. "There are three of them going to stick now!"

"He shouldn't allow that," said Lord Hastings. "He is still the commander of the vessel. He has the privilege of staying if he chooses, but he should order the others off the ship."

"He has, sir, but they refuse to go."

"Then he should insist."

"He's even threatened them, sir. But they won't go."

"Well, it's their funeral," said Lord Hastings briefly.

The German commander had now given up his attempt to force the others to leave the ship; and the three men stood quietly upon the bridge, awaiting the end.

And it came suddenly.

The German battleship suddenly seemed to leap clear of the water — the result of a second explosion, the sound of which was again barely audible to those aboard the D-17 — and came down in twain. The afterpart of the vessel disappeared beneath the water almost immediately, but in some unaccountable manner, the portion forward still floated. It was upon this that the three officers stood.

Each man stood erect, his face tilted a trifle toward the sky. The huge flashlights from the other vessels in the harbor lighted them up plainly, and Frank could see that each of the three was smiling.

Slowly now what was left of the battleship sank, the center of a broad circle of brilliancy. Down, down. Now the water had reached almost to the bridge. Now the officers stood in water up to their knees. Then the wreck dived.

Frank relinquished his place at the periscope to Lord Hastings, remarking:

"Well, she's gone; and three brave men with her."

There was no reply to this remark.

Suddenly the water close to the D-17 splashed violently. Lord Hastings looked about sharply. Again the water was kicked up, this time on the starboard how.

"They've spotted us," said the commander of the D-17. "Every ship in the fleet is bearing down on us. Submerge to five fathoms, Mr. Templeton."

Jack repeated the command and the D-17 dived.

"Now what, sir?" asked Frank.

"It's too risky to tackle any more of them," was the reply. "We'll make for the Kiel Canal."

"The Kiel Canal?"

"Yes; we are headed for the Baltic."

"But— —" began Frank.

"You will do well to remember," said Lord Hastings, "that sometimes I keep my plans to myself."

CHAPTER VIII.

IN THE BALTIC.

"Great Scott! What was that?"

It was Frank who spoke. He picked himself up from where he had been thrown by a violent shock and rubbed his head ruefully, glancing at Lord Hastings quietly the while.

Lord Hastings also had been hurled against the side of his cabin, as had Jack, who also was now regaining his feet.

Lord Hastings' reply was brief, and it was not an answer to Frank's question.

"Submerge quickly, Mr. Templeton!" he ordered.

Jack gave the command.

Lord Hastings stepped to the tube that connected with the engine room. A voice came back to him.

"Hello?" it said.

"Any damage to the engines, Jarvis?" asked Lord Hastings.

"None, sir," was the reply.

"Anybody hurt?"

"No one but me. Head bruised a bit, sir, by being thrown against the boiler. Nothing serious, sir."

"All right."

Lord Hastings stepped from the tube.

"Now," he said to Frank, "I'll answer your question. While I can't say for sure, my guess would be that, in rising, we came up under an ice floe or an iceberg. That would account for the shock."

"By Jove!" Jack ejaculated. "I hadn't thought of such a thing."

"Nor had I," said Lord Hastings, "but I should have thought of it. At this time of year it is no uncommon thing for large icebergs to be floating about in the Baltic. I am sure that is what is wrong."

"Then what shall we do, sir?"

"Well, we'll have to run on a ways. When we are from beneath the berg, we shall try again to get to the surface."

He gave the signal for ten knots ahead.

The D-17 had passed through the Kiel Canal without difficulty, in spite of the German belief that such a feat was impossible; and this German belief persisted in spite of the fact that Lord Hastings and his two young officers had performed such a feat once before – and the Germans were aware of it. Apparently, however, the enemy was confident a second attempt would never be made.

It was a long time ago now that the perilous trip had been made, but all three remembered it well. They had spoken of it often as the submarine made its way along slowly, a keen lookout being kept forward for mines or other obstructions.

Half an hour later Lord Hastings decided that the D-17 must have passed from under the iceberg, or whatever it was that had barred the vessel's attempt to come to the surface.

"We'll try it again, now," he said briefly.

In response to his commands the pumps began to work very slowly, for Lord Hastings had no mind to crash into an obstruction with the same force as before.

"The vessel might stand it and it might not," he explained as his reason for his caution. "There is no need testing the strength of our shell unless absolutely necessary."

"Don't you think she could force her way through, sir?" asked Jack.

"It all depends," was his commander's rejoinder. "It depends upon the thickness of the ice above."

The D-17 rose gradually; then, with a slight grating sound, she paused suddenly.

"Bumped it again," said Frank.

Lord Hastings nodded.

"Must be quite an iceberg," was Jack's comment.

"Unless the sea is frozen over solidly for a considerable distance," supplemented Lord Hastings.

"But that could hardly be," protested Frank.

"Oh, yes, it could. It has happened more than once; and for that reason it may possibly happen — or have happened — again."

"Then what is our next move, sir?" asked Jack.

"We'll proceed under water a ways and then try again. If we don't come up next time, we'll try and force our way to the surface. We've got to get up for a look around, and the sooner the better. The ice is likely to grow thicker with each succeeding minute."

Again the D-17 proceeded under water for perhaps half an hour and then Lord Hastings announced his intention of trying to rise.

The result this time was the same. After ascending several fathoms, the submarine encountered ice and stopped.

"Well, there is no help for it," said Lord Hastings. "We'll have to try and break through. Submerge to ten fathoms, Mr. Templeton."

Jack repeated the command and the D-17 dived deeper. At the proper depth, the vessel's course was checked. Then Lord Hastings ordered that the craft be brought to the surface with as much force as possible.

The water was sent from the tanks with a rush and the D-17 seemed to leap upward. A few moments later there was a violent shock and all aboard were thrown from their feet. The submarine had failed to break through.

"Again!" cried Lord Hastings and gave the signal to submerge.

A second attempt met with no better result and Lord Hastings immediately commanded a third trial.

"We'll have to get through now or we'll probably drown," he said quietly. "I am afraid we have strained our seams. We'll need an overhauling immediately we put into Petrograd—if we are fortunate enough to get there."

"And what do you suppose has happened to our periscope?" demanded Frank.

"Oh, that has been smashed to bits before now," said Lord Hastings quietly. "However, we can rig up another one if it is necessary before we get to port."

"All ready for the next trial, sir," Jack put in at this juncture. "We are down five fathoms."

"All right. Let her go," replied his commander.

This time the D-17 rose even more swiftly than before. Again there was a violent shock, followed by a crashing sound; and then the submarine floated clear.

"Hoorah! We're up, sir," shouted Frank.

"Don't crow too soon," was the reply. "We may be up, but there is no telling yet what condition we are in. We'll go on deck."

Lord Hastings led the way and the two lads followed closely behind him.

Outside a strange sight met their gaze. To the north, to the south and to the east and west, as far as the eye could reach, there was nothing but ice. True, it was broken in places, but it was none the less ice. The D-17 was hemmed in closely on all sides.

Jack expressed the sentiments of the others with a long whistle.

"Now, what do you think of that?" he said.

"I think it's pretty tough, if you are talking to me," was Frank's reply. "We can't push through that."

"No; and we can't stay here and wait for it to thaw," declared his chum.

"Well, then what?" asked Frank.

Lord Hastings, who had not spoken up to this moment, now broke his silence and said:

"Never give up the ship, boys. While there's life, there's hope."

"And have you a plan of some kind, sir?" asked Jack eagerly.

"Well, I have something that might be called a plan. If you look closely you will see that a hundred yards ahead there, there is what appears to be a lane—where the ice is broken. Do you see it?"

"Yes, sir," replied both lads in a single voice. "But the ice between the D-17 and that spot is solid."

"So it is. What we shall do is to dive, shape our course for that particular point and try to come to the surface there."

"And what good will that do, sir?" demanded Frank. "The chances are that the ice beyond that point is just as thick as it is here."

"We'll find that out when we get there," said Lord Hastings. "Let's go below."

They did so. The conning tower was immediately sealed, and the submarine submerged to a depth necessary to avoid any points of ice that might be likely to protrude beneath the water.

Lord Hastings had gauged the distance accurately, and when he again gave the command to come to the surface, the D-17 rose gently, pushing the loosely formed ice to both sides as her nose appeared from the deep. Lord Hastings and his two young officers immediately went on deck again.

"By Jove!" said Frank after a quick glance around. "The ice doesn't seem to be so thick dead ahead."

"You see," said Lord Hastings with a smile, "a little perseverance will go a long ways sometimes. Now, according to your reasoning awhile back, there was really no use in trying to reach this spot. But now that we are here you see still further hope. Remember that there is always a fighting chance, no matter how great the odds against you."

48

"I'll remember, sir," replied Frank.

"I hope you will. Now we'll try our luck at forcing a passage through the ice."

"In what way, sir?" asked Jack.

Lord Hastings' next words were explanation enough.

"Full speed ahead!" he ordered.

In response to the command, the D-17 dashed straight at the ice ahead. Her sharp, steel nose plowed into it with violence, and the ice, thick though it was, parted and the D-17 edged through as swiftly as could be expected.

"By Jove! I didn't think she'd do it, sir," Jack exclaimed.

Lord Hastings smiled a bit.

"I am not sure that she can keep it up without straining something," he said. "But it is better to be on the move than lying still. The ice won't part for us of its own free will, that's sure."

Still the D-17 plowed slowly along; and then, perhaps half a mile from the starting point, she stopped.

"Back her and try again," was Lord Hastings' command.

This was done and again the vessel made headway.

This process was repeated time after time; and some five hours later, those upon deck made out clear water beyond, though there was a considerable expanse of ice to penetrate.

Undaunted, Lord Hastings continued to force the D-17 against the apparently impenetrable barrier; and at last the D-17 broke clear.

Lord Hastings gave a sigh of relief.

"Now for Petrograd at full speed," he said. "We'll have a look over the ship as we go along.

There is no need stopping to do it here. Every minute may be precious. Take the wheel, Mr. Chadwick, while I make a tour of inspection."

Frank did so, and Lord Hastings turned to Jack with this command:

CHAPTER IX.

ASHORE.

In spite of the fact that, upon investigation, Lord Hastings found the D-17 leaking in several places, serious trouble in the engine room and other minor wounds suffered in her battle with the ice, the submarine made Petrograd safely and under her own steam.

It was broad daylight of the following day when the vessel sighted land. At the same time a Russian man-o'-war, sighting the D-17, immediately cleared for action and gave a signal for the submarine to heave-to. Lord Hastings obeyed and a launch put over the side and came toward the D-17. A few moments later Lord Hastings and a Russian officer were closeted in the former's cabin aboard the submarine. When they emerged, the D-17 proceeded.

Several hours later found Lord Hastings, Frank and Jack ashore, the D-17 having been turned over to the Russian naval authorities for repair. It was found that it would be necessary to put the craft in dry dock and this meant that several weeks must elapse before the submarine could be put in commission again.

"And what are we going to do all that time, I'd like to know?" said Frank, plainly disappointed.

"Well, we might look about Petrograd a bit," said Jack with a faint smile.

"Hold on there," said Lord Hastings. "I intend keeping an eye on you fellows this time. You may remember the trouble you had on your last trip here. Nothing more like that if I can help it."

"I am afraid we won't have much of a time this trip," said Frank.

"You are afraid you won't, eh?" repeated Lord Hastings. "Well, I'm in hopes you won't, and neither will you if there is anything I can do to prevent it. To tell the truth, I am half way inclined to have you both locked up for safe keeping, until the time comes for us to sail."

"Oh, we'll be good, sir," said Frank.

"You will, you may be sure of that," returned Lord Hastings. "If you're not, you may take my word that I will have something done with you."

"And now, sir," said Jack, "will you not tell us something of the nature of the reason for this sudden trip to Russia?"

"You'll learn soon enough," was the reply. "I don't suppose you would have any objections to paying your respects to the Czar?"

"Not the slightest, sir," said Frank with a smile. "I remember once when Jack paid his respects in a manner he did not wish."

"Yes; I remember that, too," agreed his chum.

"I have no doubt that the Czar will be glad to see you again," said Lord Hastings. "He will remember he probably owes his life to you, Jack."

Jack flushed.

"I hope you will not remind him of it, sir," he replied.

"I don't believe that will be necessary," declared Lord Hastings.

Nor was it, as events transpired; and it was in this audience of the Czar that the boys learned the reason for their trip to Russia.

The Czar received Lord Hastings and his officers the moment their names were presented. When the three entered his presence, he arose quickly and came forward with extended hand.

"Why, my lord," he exclaimed, "I had hardly expected to see you again so soon." He turned to the two lads. "And these," he added, "are your two young officers who were with you before. Ah, I remember. It is to them I owe my life."

He extended a hand to each and both lads flushed. Jack, the subject of a monarch himself, dropped to one knee; but Frank, who recognized no monarch, bowed low, and remained on his feet. The Czar signalled Jack to rise and then turned to Lord Hastings.

"Am I to consider this just a friendly call, or have you anything to impart to me?" he asked.

"Both, your Majesty," replied Lord Hastings gravely. "I may as well come to the point of my mission at once."

"Do," said the Czar briefly.

"Very well. What I have to say is this: In your service—and in high standing and authority—is a man who is a traitor—a man who has sold out to our common foe, the Germans."

"So?" said the Czar, apparently no whit surprised. "His name, if you please."

"His name," said Lord Hastings with a faint smile, "will surprise you. I fear you will find it hard to believe; and had I not the proof of the man's duplicity, I should not have the courage to mention the man."

Evidently Lord Hastings' words made an impression upon the Czar. He stirred uneasily.

"Come, come," he said. "The man's name. Out with it, my Lord."

"His name," said Lord Hastings very gravely, "is Count Stephan Blowinski!"

"What!" roared the Czar, leaping from his seat. "Count Blowinski! The chief of the Russian secret police! Impossible, Lord Hastings. I would stake my life and throne upon his integrity, my lord."

"Then you would lose both, sire," said Lord Hastings gravely.

"But it cannot be!" protested the Czar of all the Russias. "Count Blowinski has been, almost, my right hand. He has served me well."

"It is none the less true that he is a traitor," replied Lord Hastings.

Realizing that Lord Hastings was in deadly earnest, the Czar became more calm.

"You must be mistaken, my lord," he said quietly.

"Would that I were, your Majesty. But I am not. I have the proof here in my pocket," and he tapped his breast.

"Then let me have it!" exclaimed the Czar. "Let me have it, man! I must know the truth of this matter at once."

Quietly and without another word Lord Hastings unbuttoned his coat and from his inside pocket took a small packet, which he placed in the outstretched hand of the Czar. Then he sat back and eyed the Czar keenly.

The Czar broke the tape that bound the package with nervous fingers, shook out the papers as nervously and cast his eyes upon the words they contained. For long minutes he pored over the several documents, his brow becoming blacker and blacker; and at last he raised his head and said:

"You are right, my lord. Nothing further than these papers are needed to convince me of Count Blowinski's treachery."

Lord Hastings bowed quietly, and the Czar, again glancing at the papers, became lost in his thoughts.

"So," he muttered to himself, "you are a traitor, eh? You, whom I have treated like a brother and whom I have showered with honors. You would betray me to the Germans. Well, you should know how we deal with traitors." He turned to Lord Hastings. "I have to thank you, my lord," he said. "I shall deal with this traitor at once."

"Sire!" exclaimed Lord Hastings, "if I may be permitted to say a word."

"Speak," said the Czar briefly.

"Then, sire, I would suggest that you do not act hastily in this matter."

"And why?" demanded the Russian ruler.

"Because, sire, the Count Blowinski undoubtedly has a strong following. He will not be deposed so easily as you imagine. If you execute him summarily, there is no telling what may result—revolution, anarchy—no man can tell. Let the man convict himself in the eyes of the people—or in his own eyes and put an end to himself."

For the space of several moments the Czar was silent, considering. When he raised his eyes again, Lord Hastings knew that his better judgment would prevail.

"You are right, my lord," said the Czar quietly. "Count Blowinski has indeed a large following, though it is my own fault that he has. I have enabled him to obtain it. Why, even now he is in Moscow attending to details of a campaign I have planned that, should it be successful, would be one of the greatest steps toward ending the war that has been taken."

"And I have no doubt that he is attending to it—in his own way," said Lord Hastings grimly.

"No doubt whatever," agreed the Czar with a faint smile. "But now what's to be done?"

"The thing to do," said Lord Hastings, "is to catch him in an act of treason; then expose him."

"Easily said," returned the Czar. "But how?"

"I may be able to help with an idea," said Lord Hastings, and continued: "Why not set a man to watch him. Let this man come beneath his eye in some peculiar manner, say, apparently as a German spy himself. Have him arrested by the count's own men and then let a demand that he see the count, reach the traitor's ears. Thinking that there has been some word sent him, Blowinski will see the man. Then this man will invent a plausible story, that he may ingratiate himself with the count. Such a story should not be hard to concoct. The rest would be a question of time only. Learning just when the count planned to take his final step, the man could communicate with you and when the time for this step came, you, knowing what he was about to do, would hold the whip hand."

"A clever idea," declared the Czar after some consideration, "if I could but lay hands upon the man. He must be one who speaks German like a native German and one whom the count could never, by any chance, have seen before. If I could only find a man equal to such a task!"

"Or men, or boys, sire," said Frank boldly.

The Czar and Lord Hastings both whirled upon him.

"What is that?" demanded the Czar.

"I mean, sire," said Frank, flushing slightly, "that my chum here and I would be only too glad to undertake such a mission. I am sure that we come up to requirements."

"Impossible!" declared Lord Hastings.

But the Czar had been eyeing the two lads keenly.

"Not at all," he said in reply to Lord Hastings' remark. "Not at all, my lord. If I can satisfy myself that these young fellows could do the work, I would ask you for their services."

"Well, I am forced to say they could do the work possibly better than any others," Lord Hastings grudgingly admitted. "In fact, I know it. But I would hate to lose them."

"But you are not going to lose them," declared the Czar. "If they are as smart as I think they are, they will come through with this thing famously."

"Indeed we will, sire," declared Jack.

"Good," laughed the Czar. He turned again to Lord Hastings. "My lord," he said, "I crave your permission for the use of these two officers of yours upon the mission you have suggested."

"I am loath to part with them, your Majesty," Lord Hastings replied.

"But for the cause?" inquired the Czar softly. "For the cause."

Lord Hastings bowed his head.

"For our cause," he replied, "I would do much. I cannot deny you, sire."

CHAPTER X.

COUNT BLOWINSKI.

"You are sure now that you know exactly what to do?" asked Czar Nicholas of the two lads several hours later.

"Perfectly, your Majesty," said Frank with a bow.

"We have our instructions well memorized, sire," Jack agreed.

"Very well. Now if you will step into the next room you will find clothing laid out for you. I have seen to all arrangements while you were discussing details with Lord Hastings."

"And you say the papers that are to be found on us are concealed in the lining of the coats, sir?" asked Jack.

"Yes; I had them prepared hurriedly, but they will pass muster. They are identical; so, when the count finds them, he will believe, as I wish him to believe, that they were sent in duplicate that he might be sure of getting one if the other was caught."

"And we are not to know the contents, sire?"

"It is not necessary," was the reply. "You will shape your course according to events as they transpire. First, you must get into the good graces of the count."

"We'll try, sire," said Jack.

The two lads stepped into the next room, where, as the Czar had said, two suits of clothing were laid out. The garments caused the lads no little wonder that they could have been procured so readily. Of coarse weave, they were, nevertheless, of unmistakable German pattern, when examined closely. There was no hint of Russian manufacture about them.

Dressed and ready, they returned to where the Czar and Lord Hastings awaited them.

"All ready, sire," said Jack.

The Czar nodded. Walking to a little cabinet at the far end of the room, he returned with two wicked looking automatics. He extended one to each lad.

"A present from my kingly cousin, Kaiser Wilhelm," he said. "May they stand you in good stead. Now, you are sure that you understand the situation perfectly?"

The lads nodded.

"Good, then. Now, I will not tell you how I shall arrange for you to be picked up by Count Blowinski. You will know in due season. All you have to do is to board the night express for Moscow. It is now dark and the train will not leave for another hour. You have plenty of time, and money for your tickets you will find in your pockets. When events have shaped themselves so that you know there will be no chance of a slip, you will let me know in some manner. Trust no agents. I leave the way to you."

The Czar extended a hand to each lad.

"Good luck to you both," he said simply.

The lads bowed and then made their way from the palace, leaving Lord Hastings behind, for it had been agreed that he should not be seen with them. They had secured directions to the railroad station and once outside the palace they turned their footsteps in that direction and walked along slowly.

"This train doesn't reach Moscow until morning," said Frank, "so we shall be able to get all the rest we need en route. I am curious to know just how we are to fall in with the esteemed count."

"So am I," Jack agreed, "but I guess the Emperor of all the Russias has a few strings he can pull without any one being the wiser. The thing that troubles me is, will we be able to fool the count?"

"It's our business to see that we do," was Frank's reply. "By the way, talking about the count, do you know that I think a whole lot of this gun the Czar gave me? I wouldn't want to lose it."

"Think you could hit anything with it?" queried Jack with a smile.

"Well, I guess I wouldn't miss very far."

"I agree with you. Having seen you shoot a time or two, I am willing to lay a small wager you will come pretty close to anything you aim at. They are pretty weapons, and that's a fact."

"I am in hopes I don't have to use it," said Frank seriously, "but I can tell by the feel of it that it is to be depended on. Yes, it's a pretty handy pocket piece."

"Here we are at the station," said Jack at this juncture. "In the future we'll do all our talking in German or French—French while we believe we are among friends, and German at other times. English is dangerous."

Frank nodded his understanding.

"I'll get the tickets," he said.

He took from his pocket a roll of bills and extracted one he felt sure—he couldn't tell positively for he knew almost nothing of Russian money—was sufficient to pay for two tickets, and approaching the window said "Two to Moscow" in French. The agent passed out the tickets and Frank tendered the bill. He accepted what change was passed to him without a word and inquired the way to the train. After some little trouble they found themselves in a second-class compartment and settled back in their seats as comfortably as possible.

"And here we shall stay until we get to Moscow," said Jack. "Then, if something hasn't turned up, we'll go straight to the best hotel. We may trust the Czar not to lose sight of us."

Frank nodded.

"Best plan, I guess," he agreed.

A short time later the train started. The two lads, much to their relief, found they were to have no fellow travelers in their compartment. They conversed in low tones until the conductor came for their tickets, but once that worthy had taken his departure, Frank said:

"Well, it's a long ride, and not knowing what is in store for us at the other end, I vote we try and catch forty winks."

"I'm with you," declared Jack.

They settled themselves comfortably and closed their eyes. Five minutes later, as the train sped on in the darkness, they slept peacefully, utterly oblivious of the danger they were in or of what the morrow might bring forth.

How long they slept neither lad could tell, but it seemed to each that he had hardly closed his eyes when he was awakened by loud voices without. Both were awake instantly and as instantly each recognized the fact that the train was at a standstill. Light streamed through the window.

"Must be Moscow," muttered Jack.

"Right you are," Frank agreed. "But why all this fuss on the outside."

"I don't know why nor what," said Jack. "If they would only talk a white man's language we might learn what it is all about."

"Or German," Frank agreed.

At this moment the door to their compartment was thrown rudely open and a uniformed figure—that of a colonel of cavalry—appeared in the doorway.

Jack drew himself up.

"What's the meaning of this?" he demanded in French. "Why do you force your way into our compartment?"

"That," said the officer, also in French, "you will learn in good time. You are under arrest."

"Arrest!" cried Frank. "And what for?"

"All in good time, all in good time," said the officer with a deprecating gesture. "Out here with you."

"See here," protested Jack, "I wish you to understand that you are talking to two French gentlemen, allies of Russia in this critical stage, and I must insist that you be more choice in your words."

"So?" queried the Russian with an evil leer. "Just to put a stop to all this foolishness, I may as well tell you that I know you for what you are. You are both German spies."

"Spies?" echoed Frank. "I assure you, sir — —"

"It's no use," declared the Russian. "You have been followed for days now. We were warned of your approach and instructed to arrest you both on sight. You will come with me now, without further talk."

Jack said a few words in an aside to Frank. Immediately the Russian officer produced a pair of revolvers, with which he covered the two lads.

"No foolishness," he said quietly. "I have a squad of my men out here. Will you come out, or must I use force?"

"I assure you you are making a grave mistake," declared Jack, "but rather than cause unpleasantness, we shall come with you until we are able to prove our identities."

"You are sensible, sir," returned the officer quietly. "Alight, please."

Jack stepped from the compartment first and Frank directly behind him. Outside, a squad of half-a-dozen men surrounded them and they were marched away. They walked down several streets and turned in toward a rather handsome appearing building. Here they were led before a figure attired in the uniform of a Russian general.

This officer heard the report of his subordinate and then commanded:

"Relieve them of what weapons they may have."

An officer felt through their pockets and removed the revolvers so recently given them by the Czar. Then the general ordered:

"Lock them up and see that they are kept safely."

Again the lads were marched down a long corridor, then down a flight of long steps into inky blackness; thence along another corridor and finally into a low and narrow cell. Here they were locked in and the officer and his men withdrew.

"Nice place this," said Frank, after their captor had taken his departure.

"Rather," agreed Jack dryly. "Doesn't look to me as though we were going to get very far with this mission."

"Come now," said Frank, "you don't mean to tell me you don't see through this?"

"See through what?" demanded Jack. "This darkness? Couldn't any one see through it."

"Oh, no," said Frank. "I mean our arrest and imprisonment."

"Of course I see through it," said Jack. "We've been spotted and the count has had us caught. Must be a leak in the Czar's palace some place."

Frank laughed.

"I should say things are working out first rate," he said calmly.

"Oh, you would. Maybe you can explain it to me then."

"Easily. This is part of the Czar's plan. Now, if I am not greatly mistaken, it won't be long before our friend, the count, shows up to see whether we are really spies; and if he is convinced we are, he'll want to hold a conversation with us."

"By Jove! I believe you're right," declared Jack. "In that event we must make the count believe we are spies of the first water. I hope we don't have long to wait."

They didn't.

Half an hour later they heard footsteps coming down the corridor. Their jailer approached, followed by a huge stature of a man with a long flowing black beard.

"Open the cell door," commanded the big man.

"Bet four cents that's the count," Frank whispered very gently.

CHAPTER XI.

THE COUNT EXPLAINS HIS PLANS.

The lad was right.

"Open that cell door," commanded the big man again.

The other made no reply, but a key grated in the lock. The big man entered the cell, then turned upon the man who had unlocked the door.

"Leave us!" he commanded sternly. "Have no fear," he added hastily, as he saw the man was about to protest. "I have my revolver here," and he tapped his belt. "I can handle these two."

The man made no further objection, but departed.

The count whirled upon the two lads.

"So!" he exclaimed. "I have captured two German spies, eh?"

"Your Excellency," said Jack quietly, "I assure you we are not German spies."

"O-ho!" laughed the big Russian. "They deny it. O-ho!"

Frank also deemed it best to keep up the pretense.

"I assure you, your Excellency," he said, "that you are mistaken in us. We are French gentlemen."

Frank purposely threw a slight German accent into his voice and the big Russian noticed it immediately.

"French! and with an accent like that?" he demanded. "Come! where are the papers you carry?"

"Papers?" echoed Jack, in well simulated surprise.

"Yes, papers. I said papers and I mean papers," declared the count. "Where are they?"

"Do you think we are fools, that we carry papers with us?" demanded Jack somewhat angrily, it seemed to Count Blowinski.

This answer rather pleased the count, for it gave him the idea that he had two shrewd young men before him. He lowered his voice suddenly.

"Come," he said. "It is all right. I am Count Blowinski. It is for me the papers you carry are intended."

Jack glanced quickly about him and the move was not lost upon the count. Still the lad seemed undecided and protested his innocence in vigorous terms, in which Frank joined. Count Blowinski laughed softly.

"I like you two," he declared. "You are cautious, which is a trait to be admired in these troublous times. But I assure you I am the man for whom the papers are intended. Give them to me. I shall see that you are released and I shall have use for you myself."

"If we could but be sure," said Jack, "then we could deliver our message."

"It is verbal, you mean?" demanded the count.

"How else?" queried Frank.

"Good, then tell me."

"If you will prove to our satisfaction that you are really Count Blowinski, we shall do so," said Jack. "I see it is useless to profess ignorance any longer."

For answer the count stepped to the door of the cell and raised his voice in a call for the jailer. The latter hurried forward.

"Tell these prisoners who I am," ordered the count.

"You are Count Blowinski, your Excellency," replied the man.

"Good," said the count. "Leave us again." The man retreated and again the count turned to the two lads: "Are you satisfied now?" he asked.

"Perfectly, your Excellency," declared Frank.

He took off his coat, and ripped open the lining. Then he produced a paper, which he passed to the count. Jack did likewise.

"They are in duplicate," said Jack. "In case one of us failed to get through, the other, it was felt, would reach you safely."

Quickly Count Blowinski scanned the papers and then tore them into little pieces and dropped the bits into his pocket.

"Now," he said sternly, "if you will tell me why you told me you carried a verbal message?"

His words were a question and Frank replied quietly.

"So that, in the event you were not really Count Blowinski, you would not know that we carried papers," he said.

"Good! Good!" cried the Russian. "You are shrewd. I shall be able to make use of you. I suppose you know that the contents of these papers put both of you at my disposal?"

"No, your Excellency, we had not been so informed."

"But it is true," declared the count. "And your courage and resourcefulness is commended to me. Yes, I shall have use for you."

"We are at your service, your Excellency," said Jack.

The count moved toward the door.

"I shall have to leave you here for a time," he said. "It may be an hour, it may be six. Things cannot be done in a minute without arousing suspicion, in spite of my rank. However, I shall have you out as soon as I possibly can, for I would converse with you further. Good-bye."

He passed out and again summoned the jailer, whom he ordered to relock the door. This done, the two moved away.

"Well, he swallowed it," said Frank, after he was sure the count was out of hearing.

"I should say he did," Jack agreed. "I didn't imagine it would be so easy."

"Nor I; but we have the hardest part of the work still ahead of us."

"And we shall carry it to a successful conclusion," said Jack.

"Or know the reason why," added Frank.

It was well within the specified time that a jailer again approached the cell and commanded the two lads to follow him.

"Where are you taking us?" demanded Jack.

"Count Blowinski desires your presence," replied the guard.

The lads followed without further questioning.

They were ushered into the count's presence in his own handsome apartments. They were rather surprised when they found the count was not alone, but their surprise was short lived, for after the guard had taken his departure, Count Blowinski addressed them immediately.

"I have this moment signed your pardons," he said. "I have told the military authorities, who are under my supervision, that I have positive evidence you are not German spies. My word goes here yet—and will in the days to come, when the German armies have occupied Moscow."

The count swept his arm about the room, taking in all the other figures in a single comprehensive gesture.

"These," he said to the two lads, "are the men who are with me in this undertaking. You may speak plainly before them."

The lads bowed to the circle of faces.

"Very well, your Excellency," said Jack quietly.

"By the way," said the count, "how am I to address you?"

Jack smiled slightly as he replied, indicating Frank.

"My companion here as Lieutenant Maurice Depree and myself as Lieutenant Raoul Santon, of the French army."

"Good," said the count. "Good for our work here. But your real names?"

"Are not to be mentioned in Moscow," replied Frank simply.

"And why?" demanded the count with a sudden show of anger.

"Because it is commanded," returned Frank firmly.

For a moment it seemed that the count was about to make an angry retort, but he checked himself and after a moment smiled.

"A command," he said, "is a command. It would be well if others obeyed orders as well as you."

He then presented each lad in turn to the various men about him, and Frank and Jack were surprised to learn that some men so high in the Russian service were engaged in this gigantic German plot.

"The names of some," thought Frank to himself, "would startle the whole world."

"And now," said the count, "perhaps you can throw a little light upon a subject we have been trying to solve. First, of course, you know something of what we are planning to do?"

"A trifle," said Jack.

"I shall explain. Our plan is to gather together, in Moscow first, such a number of men who are dissatisfied with Russian rule, as to raise a hand for the Kaiser. I may say without boasting that at this moment I have the pledges of at least a hundred Russian noblemen to use their influence and what power they have to join when the time is ripe. There is dissension among the troops, particularly those who have been held here and in Petrograd—St. Petersburg once more when German arms have been victorious. Among high officers in the army we have found recruits, as well as in the ranks. When the time comes we shall strike, and when it does come I have enough men at my command to capture Moscow and hold it.

"Now, perhaps you have heard that the Czar will visit Moscow next week?"

Frank nodded, and then he took a long chance.

"It was for that reason, so I am told," he said, "that we were sent here at this time. I can now give you what verbal instructions I carry. I am commanded to tell you that the time to strike is on the last day of the Czar's visit to Moscow, after which, it is understood at home, he is going to the front."

"Good! Good!" cried Count Blowinski. "It is as I told you, gentlemen," and he gazed at the others in the room. "Did I not tell you the time for action had come? I said it when I first learned that two German spies— —" here he smiled—"had been captured. So the time is almost here! Good!"

There were nods and low murmurs of approval from different parts of the room. Count Blowinski swept the others with his eyes.

"The time has come for you to prove yourselves," he said sternly. "Let each of you go your way now and report to me at this hour the day after tomorrow. And remember, I am still the Czar's right hand. Should a single man betray me, I shall still have the power to send him to Siberia. Be warned."

He glared at the others, who now left the room rapidly. The count signaled the two lads to remain with him.

"You gentlemen," he said after the others had gone, "shall remain as my guests. The freedom of the town and the house is yours. By the Kaiser! I am glad you have come. I was beginning to tire of waiting. Will you join me in a glass of wine?"

Frank was about to refuse, but Jack stayed him with a look.

"With pleasure, your Excellency," the lad said quietly.

The Russian clapped his hands and a servant appeared. The count gave a command in Russian and the man disappeared, only to reappear a few moments later bearing a tray on which was wine and glasses. The count filled the glasses, and as each stood with his glass raised the count exclaimed:

"Confusion to Nicholas!"

As the count threw back his head and drained the glass, each lad was able to dispose of his wine in a jardinière which stood nearby.

"Your Excellency," said Frank, "if you would be so kind as to put a room at our disposal, we would rest for a brief while. Your Excellency may never find it out, but a dungeon cell does not rest weary bones."

"To be sure," said the count with a laugh. "I had forgotten your recent hardship."

He clapped his hands for his servants, then continued: "No, Count Stephan Blowinski shall never repose in a dungeon cell!"

CHAPTER XII.

THE BOYS MAKE PROGRESS.

The two following days passed without incident. Frank and Jack remained in the palatial home of Count Blowinski as honored guests. What excuse the count had given his subordinates for releasing them and giving the freedom of the house and of the city itself, the lads did not know; it was sufficient that he had done so. They went and came without question.

It was on the evening of the third day — shortly before the supper hour — that Jack, passing the door of the count's private office, caught a word or two from within that caused him to prick up his ears. He stopped and listened.

"To-night at eight, then," came the words in a voice he did not recognize.

"To-night at eight," repeated Count Blowinski. "Be there without fail. I expect a full attendance, for it is quite likely that plans of importance will be discussed. You know the password?"

"Yes, your Excellency. 'The Czar' only spoken in German."

"Exactly; and the knock?"

"Five sharp taps, a loud tap and two short taps."

"Good. At eight then."

Jack flitted silently down the hall and turned into a room just as the door to the count's quarters opened. The lad was afraid to take the risk of trying to get a look at the count's visitor, for had he been detected, he did not know what might happen. He made his way to the quarters assigned him and Frank, where he sat down to await his chum's return.

Seven o'clock came and Frank did not put in an appearance. Seven-fifteen, and still no sign of him. Jack began to grow uneasy. Seven-thirty, and he had not returned.

"Pshaw! I guess he can take care of himself," muttered Jack.

He donned his heavy cloak, picked up his hat and descended to the street. There, in the shadow of the house, he took his stand. A few moments later,

Count Blowinski appeared in the doorway. A moment later the count's large automobile drew up. The Russian descended the steps and entered the car.

As the machine moved off, Jack rushed from his hiding place, and by a sprint, caught hold of the rear of the car and pulled himself up behind. The machine continued on its way for perhaps fifteen minutes. Jack kept careful note of the direction, that he might find his way back safely.

Then the driver turned the car into a dark and narrow street and reduced his speed. Jack dropped lightly to the ground and dashed to the shelter of the dingy buildings that lined the walks. Muffled in his huge coat, he knew he ran little risk of detection.

A short distance up the narrow street the car stopped and Count Blowinski alighted. Immediately the auto turned and sped in the direction from which it had come.

Jack slouched toward the count.

The latter took one look at the approaching figure, and then, apparently satisfied, turned on his heel and walked rapidly up the street. Jack followed a considerable distance behind but still close enough to make sure he would not lose sight of the count.

Before a single story building, even more dingy looking than the rest, the count paused. One swift glance he gave about him, and not perceiving Jack some distance behind—as the lad had slunk close to the shelter of the house, he disappeared down a flight of stairs into the basement.

Jack moved forward more rapidly now.

The lad had noticed that before Count Blowinski descended the stairway he had settled his heavy fur cap more firmly upon his head, apparently to conceal his features. Jack did likewise.

At the head of the steps—at the same point where the count had paused momentarily—Jack also paused for a second. He thrust both hands into the pockets of his great coat and made sure that his revolvers were ready. One quick glance he cast about him and started; for he felt sure that he had perceived a form lurking in the shadows some distance back.

But it was too late to hesitate now; so, drawing a long breath, Jack descended the steps.

Below he expected to find a door, where it would be necessary to give the knock he had heard mentioned in Count Blowinski's rooms earlier in the evening; but there was no door, or if there were, it was standing open. At any rate Jack did not see a door and he passed into the darkness beyond.

It was inky black inside, and Jack walked forward slowly, one hand touching the wall on the side as he advanced. Suddenly he brought up against a solid wall. He felt along in the darkness and found that the passage turned to the left. He continued along it.

Suddenly he stumbled. His foot had struck something. He leaned down to investigate and discovered that the something was nothing more than a flight of stairs. He mounted them as rapidly as the darkness would permit.

At the top he came to another passageway, leading off to the right. Down this he walked in the darkness for fifty paces and then brought up against another solid substance. He stretched out his hands on each side of him. There was no turn in the passageway. Apparently the obstruction that barred his progress was a door.

Here was where it would be necessary to knock for admittance.

Jack did not hesitate. Five sharp taps he gave, followed by a single loud tap, and then two sharp taps.

A moment later the door swung inward a trifle and a head showed itself.

"The word?" the man questioned in a deep voice.

"The Czar," replied Jack firmly in German.

"Enter," said the voice.

The door swung back farther.

Settling his cap firmly on his head, Jack once again felt of his revolvers and stepped inside. Before him another long passageway stretched out.

70

Apparently the man who had opened the door at the lad's knock was some distance from the rendezvous.

Jack asked no questions, but walked ahead.

Several more turns and another flight of stairs he traversed before bringing up before another door. Here again he found it was necessary to knock, but he ran the gauntlet safely and a few moments later found himself inside, thinking to himself as he gazed upon the circle of men who sat about the room:

"Certainly they are careful enough not to be discovered."

Within the room there were fully half a hundred men gathered about. The room was only dimly lighted and it was next to impossible for Jack to make out the features even of the man immediately next to him on either side. In spite of this, however, the lad was careful to keep his coat well up around his chin and his cap down over his ears. This attracted no undue attention, however, for it seemed to be the purpose of every man in the room to keep his identity hidden.

Apparently the meeting, or whatever it was, had not been called to order yet, for the men were simply sitting or standing about quietly. They seemed to be awaiting the arrival of some one.

And a few moments later the some one came.

A big man he was, taller and heavier than Count Blowinski himself, and he walked into the room with the air of a man born to command. He passed to the far end of the room, where he turned to face the others. Count Blowinski approached and stood by his side. The faces of these two alone were plainly visible.

A Russian was Count Blowinski, it could be told at first glance, but Jack experienced a shock of surprise when he obtained his first clear view of the other man. The latter was a German. There could be no doubting his Teutonic features. Jack wondered how he could roam about Moscow at large without being picked up by the Russian authorities.

Count Blowinski was the first to speak.

"Gentlemen," he said, "I have the pleasure to inform you that the time to strike has come. To-morrow the Czar comes to Moscow. I shall expect each one of you to do your duty. There is no need to discuss our plans. Each man here knows the work that has been assigned to him. In my pocket are all your names. The man who fails shall have me to reckon with and I assure you that Siberia is an unpleasant country.

"The Czar comes to Moscow to-morrow only with his personal bodyguard. He is relying upon me to furnish the men who shall protect him. I shall do so, though in a way that possibly will surprise him. That is, I shall do so with your assistance. If you are still with me, you will please say 'aye.'"

"Aye!" came in subdued voices from the other conspirators. Even Jack joined in.

"We shall seize the Czar," continued the count, "as he addresses his troops on the palace grounds. Aside from the Czar's personal bodyguard, the troops will be mine, carefully selected by you. I shall expect them to do their work.

"Herr von Louden here tells me that, half an hour after the time appointed for the Czar to address my troops, a fleet of half a hundred German airplanes, together with a score of Zeppelins, will appear over the city. At the same moment, a German fleet, which has pushed through the Baltic to the Gulf of Finland, will force an entrance and bombard Petrograd. Further south, the allied Teutonic armies will begin a gigantic offensive at almost the same moment. The Russian troops will be forced back upon all sides. The people will cry for peace, and I, having assumed my new role under the protection of his Majesty Wilhelm II of Germany, shall give them peace. They will thank me, and you, gentlemen, for bringing peace to our troubled country. That is all, except that Herr von Louden is present to-night to vouch for the truth of my words and to reassure you that the Emperor of Germany will keep his royal word."

The German then spoke a few words, after which Count Blowinski said:

"Now, if there are no remarks, I shall declare this meeting adjourned."

There were no remarks. Apparently no man present had anything to say.

"But before you go, to begin your respective tasks," said the count, "I shall ask each man present to pass before me and remove his hat, that I may make sure there is no traitor nor spy among us to-night. I should know the face of every man present and I should know whether he is entitled to be here. You will please walk before me on your way out."

"Great Scott!" muttered Jack to himself. "I'm in for it now. I am sure to be recognized and the count will hardly accept any explanation I may make. Worse, if discovered, I shall be unable to give the warning and the plot will succeed."

The lad's lips set grimly.

"There is always a fighting chance," he told himself quietly, remembering the remark Lord Hastings had so recently made to Frank. "Well, they'll know I have been here before I go down."

He thrust his hands into his pockets and grasped a revolver securely with each. Then he followed the line of men who were passing before Count Blowinski.

The single light in the room was right above the count's head and it fell squarely upon each man's head as he passed before the count. Behind Jack came other men.

CHAPTER XIII.

THE FIGHT IN THE PASSAGE.

A form pressed Jack closely from behind.

"Careful!" said a low voice that the lad recognized with a start.

Jack half wheeled and muttered:

"Frank! What——"

"Sh-h-h," was Frank's response, for it was really he, and added quickly: "When the light goes out, duck and make for the door. I'll be behind you."

Jack said nothing, but awaited developments as he moved still nearer Count Blowinski. He held himself tense, ready for anything that might transpire.

Frank held his right hand carelessly in his pocket as he moved slowly forward behind Jack. The long line of men were passing through the door, but there were still many more behind.

A close observer now would have seen the right side of Frank's great coat rise slowly. The hand within was pulling it up. Suddenly it flashed up still more suddenly and there came a sharp report. There was a sound of crashing glass and the room was immediately plunged into darkness.

Through his overcoat, Frank had shot out the light!

At the moment he had pressed the trigger Frank had reached forth his left hand and clasped Jack by the arm. Then he leaped in the direction of the door dragging Jack after him.

"Quick!" he cried.

For a moment after the single shot, there was a deathly stillness in the room and in that moment Frank and Jack almost reached the door. Almost but not quite. At a far end of the room a match flared up. Frank, who had now drawn his revolver from his pocket, raised it quickly and fired again. The match went out.

But this second shot had betrayed the lads' new position to the other occupants of the room. A terrific roar went up and several revolvers cracked sharply.

But Frank and Jack had been too quick for the others. Immediately Frank had fired, both had dropped to the floor. Then rising they sailed into the crowd of Russians before them with their hands, striking out right and left.

It was in this kind of fighting that Jack showed up best. Though his wits were no quicker than Frank's, his courage no greater, his blows were heavier and his weight bore all before it.

Quicker than it takes to tell it he had cleared a passage to the door, and reaching back, he grabbed Frank by the arm and pulled him through after him. Unfortunately, the door closed the wrong way, so he could not close it after him.

"Run!" he cried.

Frank needed no urging and darted after his chum, at the same time crying out:

"Look out for the steps, Jack!"

But Jack did not need this warning. Always observant, he had measured the distance from the steps to the door as he entered, and now he drew in the darkness a scant three paces from the steps. He felt for them with his foot.

"All right," he said to Frank, who had stopped when he collided with his friend. "Fifteen steps down, then run to the left."

Frank followed instructions without question.

Suddenly Jack came into contact with a figure in the darkness. The lad shoved him to one side and the two darted by. Other figures now blocked the passage. They were the men who had passed out ahead of the lads.

There were hoarse cries of alarm and surprise; but unheeding these, the two boys ran on. The advantage was theirs, for the Russians, although realizing something was wrong, could not see them and did not know the causes of all the trouble were so near.

Frank and Jack turned into the last passageway safely. And there it became light.

Before the door at which stood the first guard was a light. The guard himself, attracted by the sounds of commotion from behind, faced the lads as they turned into the passage, a drawn revolver in his hand.

"Halt!" he cried.

Without pausing in his stride, Frank raised his own revolver and fired around Jack's side. The Russian dropped.

Jack pulled up before the door.

"Pull it open!" cried Frank.

Jack laid hold of the knob and pulled. The door did not budge.

"Hurry!" cried Frank.

Came the sounds of running footsteps from behind, loud cries and shouts.

Again Jack wrenched at the knob, and it came away in his fingers. Jack looked at the knob in dismay.

"It's broken," he cried.

At that moment the first Russian hove in sight. He saw the lads at the same moment Frank perceived him. Both raised their revolvers simultaneously, but Frank was the first to fire.

"Blow the lock off the door!" cried Frank. "I'll hold 'em back."

Jack placed the muzzle of his revolver to the lock and pulled the trigger. Still the door would not open.

A second Russian came into sight in the rear. Again Frank fired with excellent result.

"Open the door!" he cried to Jack.

"It won't open," Jack shouted back.

"Blow the lock off!"

"It didn't come off!"

"Try it again!"

Jack did so; and still the door refused to budge.

"Guess I don't hit it in the right place," he said quietly.

"Well, turn around here and do a little shooting," said Frank. "Here they come. They'll try to rush us."

"We should be able to hold them," replied Jack cheerfully.

He fell to one knee, and holding one revolver in his left hand by his side, rested his right elbow on his right knee.

Two Russians appeared around the corner at the same moment.

Crack! Crack!

Just two shots and the Russians toppled over. A second pair met the same fate. Another man did not appear.

"You guard this end a moment and I'll have a try at the door," said Frank.

Jack nodded.

Frank placed his revolver against the lock and fired. Immediately the lad swung the door open.

"Fire a couple of shots to hold them back," he cried.

He suited the action to the word and Jack followed suit. Then both lads sprang through the open door into the darkness. They ran down the narrow hall as fast as their legs would carry them.

"Watch the steps!" cried Frank again.

Jack pulled up at the edge of the stairs safely and they descended them rapidly. Footsteps from behind indicated that the Russians had discovered their absence and were in full chase again.

Down the dark passageway ran the lads at full speed and at last came to the outside. Quickly they climbed the few steps to the street and ran down the thoroughfare.

"Here's where we shall have to hustle," shouted Frank. "They can spread out here and pick us off. Double around the first corner."

They did so and with better fortune than they could possibly have hoped for; for not a Russian emerged from the house while they were in sight.

"Around the next corner, and the next and the next," shouted Frank.

Jack obeyed; and after turning half-a-dozen corners the lads felt sure they had shaken off their pursuers.

"We'll have to get away from here," said Frank as they slowed down. "Count Blowinski, being in command, will have the police and military authorities scouring the neighborhood. If we are picked up in this part of town, we will be no better than if we had been caught in the house."

Turning the next corner, Jack came to a halt.

"Look!" he said and pointed.

Frank glanced in the direction indicated.

"Well," he said, "all I see is an automobile."

"Exactly," replied Jack, "and that is the thing that will get us to some other part of the city quicker than our legs."

"Right you are," said Frank. "No time to lose."

They approached the car.

"Hello," said Frank suddenly, "it's occupied."

A figure of a man had appeared suddenly in the front seat.

"It'll soon be unoccupied," declared Jack.

Frank made no reply and they approached the machine.

Jack walked directly up to the man and spoke.

"You will oblige me by getting out of there," he said in German.

The man understood, but he had no mind to give up his property so easily. He sought to temporize.

"This is my machine," he said. "By what right— —"

"By the right of necessity," said Jack calmly. "He stretched forth a long arm and grasped the man by the collar and lifted him to the ground.

"Stay there," he said. "All right, Frank. Hop in and start her off. I'll keep an eye on this fellow until you are ready."

Frank leaped in the front seat quickly.

"Luck!" he exclaimed. "A self starter. I was afraid we would have to crank her up. Leave him there and climb aboard."

Jack thrust the man from him.

"Stay away," he warned and leaped into the car.

But this Russian was no coward and he determined to fight for his property. He produced a revolver.

"Stop and get out of there!" he commanded.

Jack looked at him and sighed.

"Poor fellow," he said. "I guess it must be done. All right," he called to the man. "You've got the drop on us. We'll get out."

He suited the action to the word and got to the ground deliberately and without haste. He looked at the Russian calmly, and the man lowered his weapon. It was the moment for which Jack had been waiting, and his right hand shot out with amazing speed and an aim that was true.

Struck squarely upon the point of the jaw, the Russian crumpled up on the ground without a sound. Jack climbed back in the machine.

"All right, Frank," he said. "Let's go."

CHAPTER XIV.

FRANK TAKES A JOURNEY.

"Whew!"

Frank dropped his heavy coat on the bed and turned to Jack with a wry smile. Jack smiled back at him.

"I recognize your feelings," he said. "Pretty close and no mistake."

"I should say. Wonder if our good friend the count has returned yet?"

"I don't imagine so. Guess he'll be up half the night seeking some trace of the intruders who were so unkind as to disturb his meeting and shoot up some of his henchmen."

"Hope he doesn't look here for them," remarked Frank. "I want to get some sleep."

"To tell the truth, I wouldn't be surprised if he hunted us up the moment he comes in," said Jack. "He'll want to tell us what is coming off to-morrow, so that we may be on hand. Nice fellow, the count. Seems to like us quite a bit."

"So he does," was Frank's rejoinder. "Can't say that I return the feeling, however."

"No. Well, we'll turn in, anyhow; perhaps the count won't be so unkind as to disturb us."

"Hold on now," said Frank. "There is something else to be decided on before we can sleep."

"What's that?" demanded Jack.

"Well, we haven't communicated with the Czar yet, and he will arrive here to-morrow. How are we going to warn him?"

"Say! That's not such an easy question, is it?"

"I guess not. The count and his crowd will meet the Czar at the station, I suppose."

"Well, we can be there, too."

"Yes; but if we try to give the warning there it will spoil everything."

"Then what are we going to do?"

"That's the question. Let me think a bit and try and do a little yourself."

The lads became silent, considering the situation. It was Frank who finally broke the silence.

"I've got it!" he declared.

"Well, let's have it," returned Jack.

"All right. It's very simple, too. It's still early. There is a train to Petrograd at midnight."

"So there is," said Jack. "But you forget that it won't get you there in time to catch the Czar before he leaves Petrograd."

"Oh, no, I don't," said Frank. "I have been studying maps and things since we have been here, and I have found a certain town that is a railway division point. All trains stop there to change engines. I'll get off there and wait for the Czar's train to come through."

"Hm-mm," said Jack. "That will be some time early in the morning. If the Czar has arisen, all well and good. If not, you'll have a hard time getting to him."

"Something must be left to chance," returned Frank quietly.

"So it must," agreed Jack. "Well, in lieu of a better plan, that will have to do. Now will you go, or do you want me to go?"

"Seeing that it's my plan, I guess I'll go," said Frank.

"All right. Then you had better hurry. I'll tell the count that you have disappeared. It wouldn't do for him to find you here to-night and not in the morning."

"Right you are," agreed Frank. "Well, I hate to go, for, to tell the truth the bed looks awfully inviting. However, it's got to be done."

He slipped into his overcoat quickly and extended a hand to Jack.

"Just in case anything happens," he said quietly.

Jack grasped the hand and squeezed it.

"I'll bide here quietly," he said. "I'll probably be at the station when the royal train pulls in to-morrow. You'll probably come back with the Czar. If you get a chance, tip me the wink."

"I won't get a chance," said Frank, "for I will keep very much out of sight. If the count should see me in the Czar's retinue he would smell a mouse immediately."

"By Jove! so he would," agreed Jack. "Well, I'll find you some place when the excitement is over."

"Right. Now I'll have to hustle or the estimable count is likely to return before I make my disappearance. I'll have considerable time to kill at the station."

"I'll go to the door with you," said Jack.

"Better not. Just sit tight where you are." Frank moved toward the door. "Well, so long," he said.

"Good-bye and good luck," said Jack.

"Thanks; the same to you. Your position is more ticklish than mine. You'll have to explain my strange absence."

"Oh, I guess I can do that."

"So do I. Good-bye."

Frank closed the door behind him and hurried from the house.

Left alone, Jack immediately prepared for bed. There was nothing that he could do now and he had determined to get what rest he could, for he realized that the events of the morrow were likely to be very strenuous. He put out the light and climbed into bed. Five minutes later he was fast asleep.

How long he was asleep he did not know, but he was awakened by a pounding at the door.

"Come in," he called sleepily, when he was fully awake.

Count Blowinski entered the room and switched on the light.

"Oh, in bed?" he said. He glanced at the lad and then added: "Where is our friend Lieutenant—Lieutenant Depree?"

He smiled at the name.

"By Jove!" said Jack, sitting up in bed and looking around sleepily. "He hasn't come in yet. Wonder what can have happened to him?"

"Oh, I guess he'll show up in the morning," was the count's reply. "He is probably out looking about the town."

"Probably," agreed Jack, with a laugh. "However, he's old enough to look out for himself. Did you want to see me about anything particular?"

"Why, yes. I wanted to tell you that the time for action has come."

"Good!" Jack exclaimed eagerly. "When?"

"To-morrow."

"To-morrow? You mean the Czar will be here to-morrow?"

"Yes; and if my plans do not miscarry I shall be master of Moscow before the sun has set—and within the month Russia will have declared peace with Germany."

"That is indeed good news," declared Jack. "But you are sure there is no danger of your plans going wrong?"

"That," said the count, "is why I have stopped in your room to-night."

For a brief moment Jack's heart stood still and he thought to himself:

"Can he have discovered anything?" Aloud he said: "I shall be glad to do anything in my power for the cause."

"I was sure of it," said the count, and Jack's fears fled. "Now the situation is this: To-night we—myself and the men who are with me in this undertaking—held a meeting, where I gave my instructions to proceed with the coup to-day. Just after I declared the meeting adjourned, I decided that I would have a look at the face of every man present. They were passing before me when there was a shot and the light went out. A fight followed. There were two spies in the meeting."

"You don't tell me!" exclaimed Jack. "And have you any idea how they gained admittance?"

"Not the slightest."

"Well, it doesn't matter, I suppose," said Jack deprecatingly. "They are dead now, aren't they?"

"No," said Count Blowinski slowly; "that is the trouble; they escaped."

"Escaped!" Jack repeated incredulously. "What! you allowed them to escape?"

Count Blowinski grew somewhat angry.

"We didn't let them escape purposely, you may be sure of that," he declared.

"Possibly not," admitted Jack, "but how many of you were there in the room?"

"Well, enough to have taken them," returned the count, his face somewhat red, "if that's what you are driving at. There were possibly fifty of us."

"Fifty of you and you let two men escape?" ejaculated Jack. "Count, I fear for the success of your plans."

"But this was unavoidable," protested the count, apparently thinking much of Jack's good opinion. "They acted so suddenly and they had us at a disadvantage."

Jack decided that he had wounded the count enough. So he said:

"I can see, count, that you were at some disadvantage. But now that these men have escaped, are you not afraid that your plans may be betrayed?"

"Not at all," was the reply. "I have taken all precautions. I have ordered that no messages be accepted by telegraph companies; I have thrown a cordon around the town through which no man could pass; I have notified the railroads that no man without a passport signed by me be allowed to leave the city."

"You have done well, count," declared Jack. "But your man may slip through. Take me or my friend for example. We both carry passports signed by yourself. Why not another?"

"Because, besides the passports held by yourselves, I have signed no other."

"Then your plans are in no danger," said Jack briefly.

"Of course not. But the reason I have disturbed you to-night is that I would give you the privilege of being on my staff when I go to meet the Czar to-morrow."

"I shall be delighted, count, and I thank you for your thoughtfulness. It will give me pleasure. But, by the way, count, supposing the Czar comes in force?"

"Ah, but he will not."

"You cannot be positive on that score. He may send thousands of troops ahead of his special train. How many men can you count on?"

"Enough, I believe. Say five thousand."

"Hardly enough to seize the Czar if he comes properly attended," said Jack dryly.

"It is enough," protested the count. "It must be enough. I cannot fail now. To do so would lose me favor with the German emperor, as you know. And I should be discredited here. There would be nothing left for me in Russia."

"Nor any other place, count," added Jack.

"No, nor any other place," said the count slowly.

He turned and left the room without another word.

CHAPTER XV.

THE CZAR IS WARNED.

When Frank left Jack he made all haste toward the railway station and purchased a ticket for Klaw, the railway division point he had mentioned to Jack. It still lacked an hour to midnight and Frank paced up and down in the station. The train left at twelve sharp and Frank ascertained that it would reach Klaw five hours later, barring accidents.

At fifteen minutes to twelve Frank took his seat in a first-class compartment. Ten minutes later a guard approached and demanded to see his passport. Frank showed it to him. The guard departed.

Soon the train pulled out and when it was well under way Frank composed himself to sleep; nor did he awake until the train was on the outskirts of Klaw.

The lad alighted the moment the train came to a stop and went immediately to a hotel a short distance away. He did not wish to attract attention by making inquiries concerning the Czar's train, so he idled about the hotel, where he was fortunate enough to hear what he had expected.

"The Czar's train, I understand, will pass through soon after seven o'clock," he heard one man tell another.

It was all Frank wanted to know.

Fifteen minutes before seven Frank returned to the station, where he loitered about. A large crowd had assembled, for word of the Emperor's coming had traveled swiftly and the people had turned out to catch a glimpse of "The white father."

It was a quarter after seven when the guards began pushing the crowd back from the track. It was a sign that the royal train was near. Frank edged his way through the crowd as well as he could without drawing attention to himself. The lad realized that the surest way to spoil his plans was to attract the attention of the guards. Should they see that he was apparently too anxious to get close, they would immediately arrest him and hustle him away.

"I'll have to wait until the train stops and then take a chance," he told himself.

Came the sound of a shrill whistle from up the track. The Czar's special was approaching and the crowd cheered.

Two minutes later the train came to a stop.

The guards and what troops had been summoned were now hard put to it to keep the crowd back. Several times they charged the crowd with drawn sabers, so close to the train did they push. And then suddenly the crowd became silent.

The door to a compartment which bore the royal arms opened suddenly. Instantly two footmen stepped forward, one to either side. Three men alighted, all garbed in military costume. The last to alight was Czar Nicholas and again there was a mighty roar from the crowd.

For several moments the cheering continued and then died away as the Czar raised a hand. "The little white father" was going to address his people and the people became silent, that they might lose no word.

Quietly they listened as their Emperor addressed them in a few well chosen words; and how they cheered when he had concluded! Then the Czar turned to his two companions and the three walked up and down the platform.

Frank now found himself in the front line of the crowd; but armed guards separated him from the Czar himself, and the lad knew that it would be instant death should he attempt to approach the Russian Emperor. As they passed in front of him, however, less than thirty yards away, Frank made out that one of the men with the Czar was Lord Hastings.

He raised his voice and called in English: "Lord Hastings!"

The three figures stopped in their tracks and gazed quickly about.

Frank repeated the cry: "Lord Hastings!"

By this time guards had rushed toward Frank and seized him. Apparently they believed he was attempting to create a disturbance, for they could not understand his words.

This commotion attracted the eyes of the Czar and Lord Hastings, who moved close to see what was going on. Lord Hastings uttered a sudden exclamation of surprise and turned to the Czar.

"It is Frank Chadwick, my second officer," he exclaimed.

"So," said the Czar. "Then I shall have him brought here."

He gave a command to one of his officers and the latter approached the spot where Frank was struggling in the grasp of half-a-dozen guards. The officer thrust the men right and left, saying:

"I shall take command of this man. His Majesty desires to question him."

Immediately the guards fell back, as did the crowd, which had pushed forward to see what was going on and to lend a hand if it became necessary to quiet a man who had dared to raise his voice in the presence of the Czar.

Frank breathed a sigh of relief as the Russian officer took charge of him. He knew that he had been successful. He approached the Russian Emperor and his own commander with a smile on his face.

Lord Hastings was about to speak, but the Czar forestalled him.

"So!" he exclaimed. "This is the manner in which you perform a mission for the Emperor. I send you to Moscow and I find you in Klaw. How do you account for that, sir?"

"I have come to warn you, your Majesty," said Frank quietly.

"Warn me? Warn me of what? I had expected word from you before this."

"We have known nothing definite before," was Frank's reply, "nor have we had the opportunity of warning you. The plot against your Majesty has come to a head and the coup is to be sprung to-day by Count Blowinski."

"So?" said the Czar again. "And what kind of a plot, pray?"

"You are to be seized by Count Blowinski's troops, your Majesty, as you address them on the palace drill grounds."

"But what if I am surrounded by my own personal body guard, with twenty thousand of my own troops within call?" asked the Czar.

"Then your Majesty will be perfectly safe," returned Frank quietly.

The Czar suddenly laughed aloud and turning to Lord Hastings slapped him heartily on the back.

"Ha, my lord," he said. "Your young friend here feared that I would venture into the lion's den without weapons. He has come to warn me."

"I have done the best I can, your Majesty," said Frank, with offended dignity.

The Czar was quick to notice the change in the lad's tone and he at once felt the reason.

"Come, my lad, I didn't mean to offend you," he exclaimed. "It is just my way, as Lord Hastings here, who knows me well, will tell you. I am deeply your debtor, and your friend's. By the way, where is he?"

"Still in the count's home, your Majesty. We figured it would be unwise for both of us to leave."

"I see," said the Czar. "Long heads, as you Britishers would say, Lord Hastings. But come, our train is waiting. We shall continue our journey into the lair of my dear friend Count Blowinski."

The Czar laid a hand on Frank's shoulder and guided him toward the royal carriage. At the door, he turned to the only officer who accompanied him besides Lord Hastings.

"General Rushtriki," he said, "this young British officer and myself have important matters to discuss. He will take your place in my carriage."

"But, your Majesty," protested the astonished officer, "I—there——"

"Never mind, general," said the Czar. "I shall have my way in this; and if there is no other place for you aboard this train, well, then I guess you will have to remain here."

"I shall find another place, sire," returned the general, with ruffled dignity.

He stalked majestically away and entered another compartment.

The Czar climbed back in his compartment and motioned Lord Hastings and Frank to follow him.

"Now," he said, when he was comfortably seated and the train had resumed its interrupted journey, "now you shall tell me all about yourself, what you have been doing and what you have learned."

Frank plunged into the account of their adventures. When he told of Jack's appearance in the den of the conspirators, the Czar was moved to ask:

"And how did you find your way there?"

"Why, your Majesty," returned the lad, "I overheard a conversation in one of the hotels where I chanced to stop; and as it was too late to return and acquaint Jack with what I had learned, I took it upon myself to follow the men."

"I see," smiled the Czar. "Then you were undoubtedly surprised to see your friend there."

The conversation languished now; and soon the Czar fell asleep. Frank took this opportunity of having a few words with Lord Hastings.

"Then the Czar will not trust himself entirely to the count's troops, sir?" the lad asked.

"Indeed he will not," said Lord Hastings. "He wanted to add a thousand men to his personal bodyguard and only consented to adding the thousands upon my suggestion, backed up by his ministers."

"And there are really twenty thousand men coming, sir?"

"There are. Following this train, at ten-minute intervals, are twenty more, each carrying a thousand men. They will not reach Moscow for an hour after the royal train arrives. Then they will be disembarked rapidly and marched to the palace, where the Czar is to rest before addressing the count's troops. This, too, is my idea, for I figured that if there were to be any break it would be at that moment. A man engaged in treachery always plays to the spectacular. Then, too, if I were wrong, it could make no difference if the troops were there."

"Then your plan is not to let the count know the Czar's troops have arrived until the time for action comes, sir?"

"Exactly."

"Had I been figuring this thing out, I couldn't have done better myself," said Frank modestly. "We seem to have planned just right, sir. There is only one thing I am sorry for."

"And that?"

"That I shall have to remain behind while the Czar goes to the palace."

"And why?"

"Because, if the count saw me back with the Czar he would suspect."

"That's true," replied Lord Hastings.

"But, sir," said Frank, "if you will speak a word to his Majesty, perhaps he will grant me permission to accompany the troops that follow."

The answer for this question came from an unexpected source. The Czar had opened his eyes in time to hear the lad's words, and replied:

"You shall have the permission."

Then he turned to Lord Hastings and added with a smile. "Look from the window! You will see that we have arrived in the den of the lion. Behold the city of Moscow, where my dear friend Count Blowinski awaits my arrival with aching jaws."

CHAPTER XVI.

THE TRAP IS SPRUNG.

Troops, troops, troops. Hundreds, even thousands of men marching through the streets of Moscow drew the eyes of the populace. From the railroad station they emerged in squadrons and regiments; and the roads of all lay in the same direction — toward the palace.

Czar Nicholas and his retinue had arrived two hours earlier and were even now in the palace. It still lacked an hour of the time when the Czar was to make his address from the palace steps to Count Blowinski's own men, but these were gathered about the palace in dense masses.

The first regiment of troops to leave the railroad station and move toward the palace attracted little attention, nor did the second; but as the men continued to stream along word of their coming finally reached the ear of Count Blowinski.

That worthy, at the moment in consultation with some of his fellow-conspirators, among whom was Jack, became greatly excited when the first word reached him.

"Can it be possible that the Czar has an inkling of our plans?" he asked.

Jack took it upon himself to reply.

"It is hardly likely, count. I should judge that the presence of troops here at this time has no peculiar significance. Rather, their presence is probably part of a prearranged plan to have them go to the front. Perhaps the Czar intends to go with them."

"It may be as you say," was the reply, "but my messenger informs me that they are surrounding the palace, hemming my own men in, as though purposely."

"It does look a bit odd," Jack agreed. "But if you are afraid to go through with your plans now, count, why not postpone the coup?"

"It must be done now or never," replied the count decisively. "A delay would prove fatal. If it comes to the worst, I shall abandon my plan of seizing the Emperor and shoot him."

Jack gave a start. This was more than he had bargained for; and he realized that if the count really determined to put this latter plan into execution, there was no time to give the warning. The lad also realized that, in the event the count did try to assassinate the Czar, he, himself, was the only person who could hope to prevent it.

Jack determined, therefore, to stick close to Blowinski; and as he accompanied the count and his staff to the palace grounds to meet the Czar, he felt more certain at every step that the count's last plan was the one to be feared.

In the large open space in front of the palace stood Blowinski's own men; but even from where he stood, Jack could see the still more dense bodies of the Czar's troops hemming in those of the count. The lad could discern their attitude of hushed expectancy and he felt certain that their officers had their commands.

"It's shoot or nothing," the lad told himself, and he followed the count closely.

Now Count Blowinski approached the Czar and the latter extended a hand.

"Welcome, your Majesty," cried the count, and falling to his knee he took the hand and pressed his lips to it.

"I am glad to see you, Count," replied Czar Nicholas. "A fine body of men you have here."

"Thank you, sire! They are indeed a likely body of men and they would have you say a few words to them."

The count now presented the others of his retinue to the Czar, and followed his majesty to the top of the palace steps, as one befitting his rank and station.

There, he turned and surveyed the crowd below—a host of uniformed figures. He spoke a few words to them himself, and announced that the Czar would address them.

Then the count fell back a trifle, as the Czar advanced.

Jack watched the big Russian closely, noting that Blowinski's hand rested upon his belt, where was exposed the butt of a revolver. Jack's hand rested in his coat pocket and his fingers gripped his own weapon firmly.

"I wish Frank were here," he muttered. "I am not certain of my own aim."

Now the Czar began to speak and a hush fell over the vast assemblage.

"Soldiers!" said the Czar. "It gives me happiness to address you; and it would give me ever more happiness, were it not for one thing."

Here the Czar paused and his gaze went to the troops farther back, his own men, whom he knew could be trusted.

Jack saw the officers there exhorting their men to some sort of action as the Czar continued: "Yes, it would give me greater happiness did I not know that there are traitors among you — men who would betray me to the enemy. I— —"

What else the Czar might have said was lost in two sharp revolver reports. For a moment thereafter there was a deathly silence; followed by a tremendous uproar and the sharp crack, crack of rifles.

Jack, his eye ever keen, had been watching Count Blowinski like a hawk. As the emperor spoke of traitors, the lad saw the count's form stiffen. Then the big Russian suddenly whipped out his revolver and fired at the Czar.

But Jack had acted just as promptly. As he saw the count's revolver leap forth, the lad jerked out his own weapon. Hardly taking time to aim, but breathing a fervent prayer, Jack pressed the trigger a moment before the count's finger tightened on the trigger of his revolver.

There was not the space of a second between the two sharp reports, but Jack's revolver spoke the fraction of a second before that of the count.

Count Blowinski staggered back. The bullet from Jack's revolver had struck him in the shoulder, but his finger had already tightened on the trigger, discharging his weapon. But his aim had been deflected by Jack's bullet and the missile went wide of its mark.

Before he could fire again, had such been his intention, Jack had leaped forward and his powerful fingers were clasped about the big Russian's throat.

The force of Jack's spring had been so great that he bore the big man to the floor. At the same time he cried to the Czar:

"Back inside, quick, your Majesty!"

But the lad need not have spoken; for at the sound of the first shot, others of the Czar's personal retinue had seized their Emperor and borne him forcibly away. Then the crack of rifles filled the air.

Under the command of their officers, trapped though they were, the disloyal Russian troops turned to give battle to the loyal forces who surrounded them on all sides.

So terrific, however, were the volleys poured in on them from beyond, one after another, and so fast did they drop, that their resistance was but momentary. Yet during the time that it took them to lay down their arms and cry for quarter, fully a thousand of them were shot down.

Immediately thereafter, the commander of the loyal forces gave the command to advance, and the men came forward at the double, thrusting to right and left with their swords and long bayonets among the now unarmed men.

Jack, having choked Count Blowinski into unconsciousness, had paused a moment before going inside to watch the battle. Therefore, he was still on the palace steps when a squad of loyal troops burst through the disloyal forces and ascended the steps with a rush.

The officer in command saw Jack standing there almost alone, a revolver still in his hand, and pointing toward the lad with his sword he exclaimed:

"Seize him!"

Immediately rough hands were laid on Jack. In vain he struggled to free himself and protested his innocence of any wrong. The grasp of his captors only tightened. In spite of his struggles he was led down the steps and in among the heart of the Russian troops.

Here he was turned over to another squad of men, with orders to take him at once before General Burgoff.

Half an hour later, together with a number of Russian officers, the lad found himself before the Russian commander. The latter looked them all over carefully, then motioned to one of his men to have Jack taken out.

"He seems younger than the rest," he said. "Neither is he a Russian. I will take up his case after I have disposed of the others."

Jack was taken from the general's quarters, but he had not long to wait. At the end of another hour he was again led before the general. Besides this officer and the man who commanded the squad in charge of Jack, there was no one present.

General Burgoff leaned back in his chair and eyed Jack keenly.

"What is your name?" he demanded.

"Jack Templeton," replied Jack in English. "Lieutenant in the Royal British navy, sir."

"What are you doing here, then?" demanded the general.

"I am here on a special mission by command of the Czar," replied the lad quietly.

The Russian commander smiled into his long beard.

"A likely story," he replied.

"It is true, sir," replied Jack.

"What was the nature of this mission?" asked the general skeptically.

"My friend and I were sent here to expose Count Blowinski," returned Jack. "How well we succeeded you may see by what has just happened."

Again the general smiled skeptically.

"I hope you don't expect me to believe any such story as that?" he questioned.

"I do, sir, because it is the truth," was the lad's response.

"Well, I don't believe it. Of course, it is only natural that you would have an excuse; all men do when they are caught. It is my belief that you are one of the traitors."

"I assure you, sir — —" began Jack.

The general rose to his feet abruptly.

"Enough!" he said sternly. "Your lies will gain you nothing. I shall prescribe the same punishment for you as for the other traitors."

"But if you would only investigate my claim, sir," protested Jack.

"A waste of time," replied the general. "The Czar must not be troubled with such matters."

"You are likely to be troubled when the Czar hears of this," returned Jack quietly.

"What!" exclaimed General Burgoff. "You dare to threaten me?"

"I am making no threats, sir."

"Come, enough of this talking," said the general. "As I have said, your punishment shall be the same as that of the other traitors."

"Death?" asked Jack quietly.

"Worse," was the general's response.

Jack was surprised. What could be worse than death, he asked himself.

The answer came in an instant and a chill struck his heart, as General Burgoff said sternly:

"Siberia!"

CHAPTER XVII.

INTO SIBERIA.

If there is one country in the world where the wheel of modern progress has failed to turn, that country is Siberia. True, there is a railroad, or perhaps several railroads, that traverse and extend into the broad expanse of uninhabited country; but they are few and far between. Except in times of war, such as these, they are not much traveled.

The road to Siberia, in Jack's case, lay through Petrograd itself. There, with perhaps fifty other prisoners securely bound, he was thrown into an open freight car, bound eastward.

Muffled in his great coat, as he was, and with his heavy fur cap pulled well down over his ears, the lad was nevertheless very cold; still he was not in such imminent danger of freezing as were some of his fellow-prisoners, who, not garbed so warmly when they were arrested, shivered terribly in the frigid atmosphere.

In spite of his warm garments Jack's teeth chattered. Try as he would he could not stop them; and when the train moved off, slowly at first, and then faster and faster, it seemed that he could bear it no longer. His hands and feet grew numb, he felt his eyes closing and then he knew no more. Unconsciousness had come to his relief.

When Jack again opened his eyes it was because he felt some one kicking the soles of his feet. He tried to move them, but the effort was vain. He could barely feel the shock of the other's blows, but he realized that he was expected to get up and he knew that it would be best to obey, if possible.

Slowly the blood began to circulate through his legs and feet. They pained him sharply at first, but gradually the pain subsided and at last the lad, his hands still bound, struggled to his feet.

He took in his situation at a glance. The train had come to a stop, and Jack let his eyes rove to the north, to the east and to the south and west. Ahead was another freight car and behind another; but from the sides all the lad could see was a broad expanse of snow, stretching far into the distance. There was not a sign of a human habitation, although the lad knew that ahead probably was a railroad station, or a shed that marked a junction, or something.

Russian guards, big heavily bearded men, forced their way through the struggling heaps of humanity in the car, stirring the half-frozen men with the toes of their heavy boots. Some kicks brought groans, others curses; but, in spite of this, the men at last managed to get slowly to their feet.

Jack gazed at them curiously, forgetting for a moment his own desperate plight. The majority were men of middle age. Some were older and some few younger.

A groan at his feet attracted Jack's attention. There he saw a young boy — he could not have been more than fifteen — lying upon the floor of the car. The lad was small and delicate, half frozen, and it appeared that he could not drag himself to his feet.

But the big guard who stood over him paid no attention to the lad's pleadings to be let alone. Twice he stirred the prostrate form with the toe of his boot as Jack looked on; then, drawing back his foot, he kicked the boy heavily in the side.

The lad gave a subdued cry and rolled away. The guard moved after him and would have repeated the kick, had Jack not taken a sudden step forward, and in spite of the cords that bound his hands, placed himself before the burly guard and his victim.

"Shame on you!" cried Jack.

Jack spoke in English. Evidently the Russian, while not understanding the lad's words, guessed their import. For a brief moment he hesitated; then, drawing back his huge fist, he struck Jack a heavy blow on the right cheek.

Jack staggered, but did not fall. He stood his ground, still facing the big Russian, but there was a dark scowl on the lad's face. Again the Russian stepped forward and raised a hand.

But before the blow could fall, Jack stooped a trifle, and thrusting his head in front of him, charged. The Russian was unable to leap back in time to avoid Jack, and the lad's head struck him squarely in the pit of the stomach. The guard doubled up and fell to the bottom of the car, gasping for air.

There was a murmur of approval from the other prisoners in the car; but this was soon silenced, for half a dozen other guards, wielding revolver butts and long whips, sprang in among them, and laid about lustily. The prisoners could not fight, for their hands were bound, and there was nothing for them to do but to stand and receive the blows stolidly. But there was anger in their eyes and Jack knew that it would go hard with one of the guards should a prisoner get a hold upon him.

For himself, he bore up bravely under the biting lashes of the whip that curled about his face and legs, leaving great red welts. Eight, nine, ten times, a whip wrapped around him; then, apparently thinking the lad had had enough, the guard who had attacked him desisted.

Jack, braced for still another blow, staggered forward as the man drew back, and evidently believing that the lad was about to attack him, the Russian quickly drew a revolver, reversed the butt and struck Jack over the head. It was a hard blow and the lad fell forward on his face. Once, twice, he tried to regain his feet. Then a wall of blackness descended upon him again and he knew nothing more, while the Russian turned his attention to the other prisoners.

When Jack returned to consciousness the first thing to call itself to his attention was the warmth. His last remembrance was of cold. He tried to think, but for the space of several moments he could not piece together the tangled chain of events that revolved and revolved in his mind.

At length, however, as he took additional note of the pleasing warmth and realized that his feet were no longer numb; that his ears were not frozen and that he could breathe without the sensation of snuffing ice. He was able, piece by piece, to recall what had transpired.

"By Jove!" he said at last. "By rights, I should be lying in an open car and freezing while some great brute of a Russian stood over me with a whip. Wonder where on earth I am?"

He raised himself on one elbow and looked around, but he could see nothing. The place in which he found himself was pitch dark. The lad thought he could now catch the sound of other voices, and he called out:

"Anybody here?"

The lad spoke in English and there was no reply. He asked the same question again, this time in French, and still there was no answer. A third time he tried it, this time speaking in German. He drew an answer at last.

"Yes; Boris Duttsky. Who are you?"

Jack introduced himself in German and in the darkness, and then added;

"Where are we?"

"Siberia," was the brief response.

"I know that," said Jack. "But where are we right now? And what makes it so awfully dark in here?"

"We are in a dungeon," was the reply. "I recognize a dungeon by the feeling, because I have been in a dungeon before. I believe I know who you are. You are the English prisoner, are you not?"

"Yes," replied Jack.

"I thought so. I spotted you in the freight car when you knocked the guard down. That's why you're here."

"And are we the only two in this place?"

"I guess so. I have heard no other voices."

"And you say I am here because I knocked the guard down?"

"Yes; they consider you a bad customer."

"And why are you here?"

"For the same reason. I followed your example in the car and butted a guard under the chin. I wish I hadn't now. It's a bad business."

"Why? All they have done is lock us up where it is dark."

"Wait; in the morning they'll take us out and give us the lash."

"The lash?"

"Yes; probably lay a dozen strokes across our bare backs with their big whips. After that they'll give us bread to eat and water to drink; and that's probably all we'll get for a week."

Jack shuddered. Then he straightened himself up in the darkness.

"They had better not lay a whip on me," he said quietly.

The Russian laughed aloud.

"Why? What will you do?" he asked.

"I'll fight. I'll rush the man who strikes me, whether I'm bound or not."

"That would be foolish. The punishment would only be redoubled. No; take my advice, and grin and bear it."

"I don't know but what you're right," said Jack after some consideration. "I'll take your advice, then, in part. I'll bear it, but I won't promise to grin."

"Now that's the way I like to hear a man talk," declared the Russian. "You are a man after my own heart. It will hurt, of course, but it won't kill. Although," he added as an afterthought, "I don't know but it would be well to kill a man at once, rather than to kill him by inches as they do here in Siberia."

"You talk as though you knew something about it," said Jack.

"I do. I had a brother who was once imprisoned in Siberia, through a mistake. He was later released by the personal order of the Czar; but in the time he was here he endured much. He has told me many tales of the cruelties of the guards and their officers."

"Well, all we can do is hope that we shall have a chance to escape," said Jack.

"No chance of that—without outside help," declared the Russian. "Besides, if you were able to get away, where would you go? You are miles from a railroad and you would perish of cold or of hunger before you got far."

"The railroad can't be so very far," Jack protested. "It was only a few hours ago that we were in a freight car."

"A few hours," ejaculated the Russian. "It has been all of twenty-four."

"Twenty-four," exclaimed Jack. "Do you mean I have been unconscious all that time?"

"You must have been. And it was a blessing that you were. You saved yourself a hard walk through the snow. You were carried on a sleigh while the rest of us were forced to walk."

"Then there is no escape?"

"A man escaped once," returned the Russian grimly. "There was no pursuit, for there was no place he could go without food, as he had gone. He was found a month later in the snow. There wasn't much left of him."

Jack shuddered.

"Not for me," he said aloud.

"No," continued the Russian, "there is no chance of escape; and for that reason the prisoners are not even bound. No, without outside help, no man ever escapes from Siberia."

"Then," said Jack quietly, "we must have outside help."

CHAPTER XVIII.

PRISON FRIENDS.

The conversation languished now; and a few moments later the deep breathing of the Russian proclaimed that he was asleep. But there was no more sleep for Jack; he had slept until he could sleep no more. For long hours he lay there in his corner thinking.

"I've been in some queer and peculiar places," he told himself, "but this is the limit; also, as this Russian says, it's not going to be an easy job to get out of here."

In the darkness of the dungeon it was impossible to tell whether it was day or night outside. Jack had lost all track of time. He felt in his pockets. He had no matches and his watch and what money he had had were gone.

"They've cleaned me out pretty well," he muttered.

Several hours later Jack heard the Russian stirring about again and came to the conclusion that the man was awake. He hailed him.

"Yes, I'm awake," came the reply.

"Do you have any idea whether it is day or night?" asked Jack.

"Can't be daylight yet," was the reply. "They'll have us out of here as soon as it is light."

"Well, I wish it would hurry and come then," said Jack. "I would like to get out of here."

"So would I; but I'd rather lie here peacefully than to face what we must face when we get out."

"You mean — —"

"The lash," replied the Russian calmly.

Again Jack shuddered. The word had an ugly sound.

It seemed only a short time later when a hand was heard fumbling at the lock of the door to the dungeon. Jack and the Russian got to their feet, and then the lad realized that not even his feet were bound. He walked up and down in the darkness several times, with hands outstretched that he might not bump into a wall.

Now a streak of light pierced the darkness and Jack made out a door at the far end of the dungeon. There came a hoarse hail, and although the words were unintelligible to Jack, he supposed that they were a summons to come out. He approached the door, the Russian behind him.

Outside the door Jack and the Russian were surrounded by a squad of soldiers, fur clad. Then they were marched into the open. Here, for the first time, Jack discovered that his great coat was missing. He had not noticed the fact before, but the extreme cold now called it forcibly to his attention. He shivered.

In spite of the cold, however, Jack glanced around eagerly as he was led along. On several sides were large rock structures. Men went in and men came out. All were heavily clad and were, apparently, soldiers.

A short distance farther on, however, they came upon a group of figures who were not soldiers. These were prisoners, and they were not clad so warmly as were their captors. Most of them shivered and quaked with the cold. Jack, fresh from the warmth of the dungeon, eyed them pitifully.

Old men and young, girls and women there were in abundance; and upon each countenance was the same expression—that of fright. They were plainly subdued and cowed.

Straight toward this group Jack and the Russian were marched by their guards. There they were halted and herded into line like a lot of sheep, while their captors drew an armed circle about them. Directly there approached a man taller and more handsomely garbed than the others. This man Jack took to be the commander of the outpost. It transpired that he was right, for the big man was General Surgoff, commander of this particular prison camp.

The big officer eyed the prisoners closely; then he signaled one of his soldiers. In response to the signal, the man hurried away, to return a few moments later with two other stalwart fellows, each armed with great black whips.

The general motioned to a man foremost among the group.

One of the guards thrust the man forward. He approached the general, plainly cowed. The officer spoke a few words to him; then turned to the men with the whips.

"Ten lashes!" he ordered.

The words were hardly out of his mouth when the first lash fell upon the man's shoulders. He uttered a moan of pain, but he did not cry out. Again and again the lash fell; until the ten blows had been delivered. Then the prisoner stumbled back to his place.

Jack grew sick at the sight.

The next man summoned before the general was the Russian who had occupied the dungeon with Jack. The man went forward quietly and with an air that impressed the lad with its courageousness. Again there were a few short words and the officer ordered:

"Ten lashes!"

The Russian made no move as the first whip descended across his shoulders. He took the next blow unflinchingly and the others that followed, and returned to his place without a word.

All this time Jack had been standing within a few feet of the place where the whipping had taken place. He had stuck to the spot, for he knew it would be unwise to show any sign of weakness or fear.

The next to face the general was a woman. Perhaps her age was thirty, perhaps fifty. From her face, so care-worn and haggard, it was impossible to tell. A few words the general held with her, too, then turned to the men who wielded the whips.

"Five lashes!" he ordered quietly.

The woman uttered a piteous cry and fell on her knees, raising an appealing hand to the general. She was in this position when the first blow fell.

The arm of the second man was now raised and descended; but before the lash could find its mark, Jack sprang suddenly forward and caught the blow upon his left arm. With a cry of rage he leaped upon the man who had wielded the whip and snatched it from his hand with a single movement; then he leaped back and struck the man squarely across the face.

The man staggered back.

The second whip-wielder rushed upon the lad, with his weapon raised. This blow, too, Jack caught upon his arm. Before it could be repeated, he had dealt the Russian a heavy blow across the face, and, following it up quickly, snatched the whip from the man's hand.

Then, still furious, the lad wheeled upon the officer, who had stood by, smiling the while. As Jack faced him, the officer, still with a smile on his face, drew a revolver and pointed it squarely at him.

So great was his anger, however, that Jack either failed to see the revolver pointed directly at him, or else he was too enraged to heed it. Ignoring the weapon as though it had been no more than a toy pistol, he leaped forward with a cry.

There was a flash and a sharp report and Jack felt something burn the left side of his head; but the bullet did not stay him. Before the officer could fire again, the lad was upon him, the whip in his right hand held high above his head.

"Swish!"

It descended with all the power of Jack's good right arm.

The blow caught the general about the shoulders and he staggered back, at the same time seeking to bring his revolver again into use.

But Jack was too quick for him. Again the heavy lash rose and fell and yet again. Three times General Surgoff attempted to raise his revolver and fire and each time he was unsuccessful.

As each blow fell the general cried aloud in pain and fear.

Suddenly, tiring of his attempts to get a shot at the lad, he turned and fled.

Jack, with a grim smile on his face, ran after him.

"Swish!"

Again the lash wrapped itself around the officer's shoulders and he gave a cry of pain.

"Swish!"

This time the lash caught him in the back of the head and entwined itself about his face.

Another howl from General Surgoff.

Raising an arm in an attempt to shield his face, the general lost his balance and fell to the ground. Leaning over him, Jack seized him with his left arm and jerked him to his feet. Then, thrusting him off at arm's length, he again brought the lash into play.

"Eight!" he counted aloud.

"Nine!"

"Ten!"

He threw the lash suddenly to the ground and turned to face the squad of soldiers who came running up.

These men had been afraid to fire for fear of wounding their commander; but now they laid rude hands on Jack and held him, as General Surgoff arose slowly to his feet and felt his face and shoulders tenderly.

The officer turned an angry glare on Jack and he said very quietly:

"I should have you killed. But I won't. It would be too easy a death. You shall have twenty lashes every morning and nothing but bread to eat and water to drink for thirty days. Strip him, men!"

Jack's coat was quickly stripped from his shoulders. His vest was jerked away and his shirt ripped off. Then, his back bare, he was pushed into the center of the crowd of soldiers.

The general now summoned the two men who had first held the whips and they seized their weapons eagerly, for each had felt the weight of Jack's anger.

"Twenty lashes!" cried the general. "Ten from each of you!"

Jack braced himself to receive the first blow. It came a moment later with a terrible whishing sound. The lash wrapped itself around his bare shoulders and the pain of it was terrible.

But Jack made no outcry.

The second man delivered a hard blow, which also caught the lad about the bare shoulders, only from the other side. The lad staggered a trifle, but kept his feet with a visible effort.

A third and fourth blow came in rapid succession; and Jack staggered first to the right and then to the left. It was almost more than flesh and blood could stand.

The rawhides continued to fly with renewed vigor. Jack, who had at first kept track of the strokes, had lost all count now. He was doing his best to remain on his feet; and he kept his lips shut firmly to keep from uttering a cry of pain.

With the fifteenth blow Jack was all but unconscious, but he was still on his feet. At the seventeenth he reeled and all but fell. At the nineteenth he stumbled, and with eyes closed, fell face forward on the ground.

He did not feel the twentieth blow, for consciousness had left him.

The men who had plied the lashes, stepped back, tired out with their exertions. But they eyed Jack with a certain degree of respect.

During the terrible ordeal, not a sound had escaped his lips.

CHAPTER XIX.

FRANK STARTS TO THE RESCUE.

After Count Blowinski's attempt on the life of the Czar had failed, it was several hours before Frank and Lord Hastings found themselves in the presence of the Russian Emperor. They had kept out of sight immediately after the Czar's arrival in Moscow, for all feared that should the count chance to see the lad, it would spoil everything. Therefore, when they were summoned to the Czar's presence, it was to find Count Blowinski there as well, though disarmed, nursing a wound in his shoulder and guarded by a squad of troops.

"I have summoned you, my lord," said the Czar, "so that your officer here, Mr. Chadwick may confront the count, and thus prove to him the uselessness of further denials."

He signaled to Frank and the boy stepped forward. Approaching close to Count Blowinski, Frank gazed at him quietly.

"Have you anything more to say, Count?" asked the Czar, with a cold smile.

"Nothing," was the sullen response, "except this."

Before any one could realize what he was up to, the count leaped forward, and, throwing his left arm around Frank's neck, struck him heavily in the face three times.

In vain the lad struggled to release the grasp. The count's hold was like a grip of iron.

The Russian troopers sprang forward at a word from their officer and laid hold of the count, who struggled viciously and clung to Frank's neck tenaciously.

But the grip of the soldiers told at last and the count was dragged away, muttering fierce imprecations to himself.

"You see, my dear Count," said the Czar softly, "it is no use. You have played right into my hands; and now that you have played, you must pay the piper."

"I assure your Majesty — —" began the count, straightening himself up and maintaining an air of ruffled dignity.

"Tut, tut, Count!" protested the Czar, with a wave of his hand. "Why deny what is so plainly apparent. You are guilty and I know it. Why, I have had proof for days. I just laid this little trap to catch you as you were about to strike. But, my dear Count, I assure you that after this, your claws will not be sharp enough to scratch. What do you say, Count, shall it be death or Siberia?"

"You do not leave me much choice," replied the count, having regained his composure and facing the ruler calmly. "Let it be death."

"In that event," said the Czar, "it shall be Siberia."

"Your Majesty — —" again began the count.

The Czar silenced him with a wave of his hand.

"Take him away," he commanded the officer in charge of the squad.

Struggling and kicking frantically, Count Blowinski was dragged from the room.

"Now," said the Czar to Lord Hastings, "I can breathe easier. His very presence had polluted the air. Come. We shall return to my suite."

He arose and the others followed him from the room.

Alone with the Czar, and Lord Hastings, Frank was moved to ask:

"And what do you suppose has become of Jack, sir?"

"By Jove! I don't know," said Lord Hastings. "He should have turned up by this time."

"Well, he hasn't, sir," replied Frank quietly.

"No. Suppose you take a run over to your rooms and have a look for him," instructed Lord Hastings.

Frank disappeared, but returned a few moments later announcing that he could find no trace of his chum.

"Strange!" said the Czar. "But wait. Perhaps he was wounded in the fighting. I shall summon General Burgoff. By this time he will have a list of the injured. He may know something of him."

The Czar immediately despatched an orderly for the general, but it was half an hour later before the officer arrived. In that time Frank's uneasiness had increased to a certainty that his chum was in danger of some kind.

"General," said the Czar, when the officer stood before him, "I am seeking information of a young Englishman, who was in the city when I arrived."

"An Englishman?" repeated the general. "There may be many here, Sire."

"So there may," the Czar agreed, "but only one like the one I am seeking. He has been living with the Count Blowinski for some days. I had thought that he would be with the count. In fact, I saw him just before the trouble occurred. He stood near the count on the palace steps."

"Oh," said the general, "was he big and young?"

"Yes," said the Czar, "he was big and young."

"And you say, Sire, that he was in league with Count Blowinski?"

"Well, I didn't say so," returned the Czar, "but if you know anything of the Englishman, tell me at once."

"I am sure he was in league with Count Blowinski," said the general. "If the Englishman is the one to whom I refer, he is now on his way to Siberia."

The Czar came to his feet with a jump.

"What's that?" he demanded, thinking he had not heard aright.

"I say he is on the way to Siberia, Sire," replied the general.

"And why is he on the way to Siberia, may I ask?" demanded the Czar, his voice very calm.

"Because I ordered him sent there, Sire. I found him on the palace steps flourishing a big revolver, and I had my men seize him. He offered me some strange story for his presence there; but I knew he was lying. I had him transported to Siberia along with a hundred other prisoners at once."

"Oh, you did," said the Czar. "By any chance, did this Englishman tell you that he was engaged on a mission for me, General?"

"He did, Sire. But, of course, I didn't believe any such story as that."

"Of course not, General; as you say. But did you think of taking the trouble to investigate his story?"

"Of course not, your Majesty. I knew you did not wish me to take up your valuable time that way. Have I done anything wrong, Sire?"

"Nothing," said the Czar, "except to send to Siberia a British naval officer, a youth, who, by risking his own life, has saved your country and your Czar."

Now it was the general's turn to be astonished. He stepped back in alarm.

"You mean he was telling the truth, Sire?"

"I do."

The general clasped and unclasped his hands nervously.

"And," the Czar continued, "unless he is back here within twenty-four hours, you shall be relieved of your command, General."

The Czar spoke very softly, but the general could see that he was in deadly earnest, and his face grew pale.

"I fear it is impossible, sire," he said at last. "I have instructed the officer in command of the prisoners, to let no one approach them for any reason whatsoever. Even a telegram would not catch them now, sire."

"Then, General, you are in a difficult situation," said the Czar quietly. "And yet I will give you another chance. I shall relieve you of your command temporarily and you shall go after this young Englishman yourself. Bring him back to me safely. Here," and the Czar turned and scribbled a few words on a piece of paper, after which he affixed his seal, "this order, for the moment, appoints you commander-in-chief of all the forces in Siberia. Bring this young Englishman back to me safely, or suffer the consequences."

The general took the paper the Czar extended to him.

"It shall be done, sire," he said quietly.

"And," the Czar continued, "you will make careful inquiry. If the young Englishman has been ill treated, you will seek out the man who is the cause of this ill treatment, arrest him and bring him to me, be he who he may. Yes, even if it be General Surgoff himself!"

Again the general bowed.

"Your Majesty," said Frank at this juncture.

The Czar eyed him in surprise and Lord Hastings disapprovingly. But Frank was not abashed.

"Your Majesty," he said again.

"Well?" said the Czar.

"Can I not go with the general, sire?" he asked. "I would like to go to Jack's aid as fast as possible. He will expect me. He would hunt me out, no matter where I was."

The Czar looked at Lord Hastings.

"What do you think, my lord?" he asked.

Lord Hastings shrugged his shoulders.

"As you please, your Majesty," he replied. "I have no doubt Mr. Templeton would be glad to see him. Neither have I any doubt that Mr. Chadwick here might come in handy."

The Czar turned to General Burgoff.

"What do you think, general?" he asked.

"Well, sire, to tell the truth, I would rather not be bothered with excess."

"In that case, general," said the Czar, with the suspicion of a twinkle in his eye, "and as you have been somewhat lax in your own duties, I shall allow the lad to accompany you. You will see that he is well treated."

General Burgoff bowed low.

"It shall be done, sire," he said.

"Very well. Now, general, you will take with you from Petrograd enough men to assure you that your orders will be obeyed, come what may. Do I make myself clear?"

"Perfectly, your Majesty. I shall take sufficient men."

"And one thing more, general," said the Czar firmly. "Let me impress upon you the utter necessity of being in the right hereafter, before you take too much upon yourself. Men have been shot for less."

The general accepted this rebuke with a bow and a flush of the face.

"I shall obey, sire," he replied.

"Good. Now, make what haste you may. That is all."

The general saluted stiffly, motioned to Frank to follow him, turned on his heel and stalked from the Czar's presence.

Frank stopped a brief moment for a word of farewell to Lord Hastings and then expressed his thanks to the Czar.

"There, there!" said the latter with a laugh. "No thanks are necessary. I am glad to give you a chance of seeing Siberia with an opportunity of coming back. Run along now."

Frank hurried after General Burgoff. And as he moved quickly along he muttered to himself:

"Poor old Jack! All alone away up there in Siberia. I'll bet he is having a terrible time and looking for me. Well, I'll be there before long, Jack, old boy!"

CHAPTER XX.

CRUELTY BECOMES UNBEARABLE.

"That's enough. I'll save the extra lashes until he is in a condition to feel them. Take him back to his dungeon."

It was General Surgoff who spoke. He looked down upon the prostrate form of Jack, who, shirt again stripped from his shoulders, had fallen beneath the terrible blows of the lash in his second whipping.

It was at the tenth blow that Jack had fallen forward on his face, unable to bear the pain any longer. General Surgoff decided that it was useless to waste blows on an unconscious enemy, so he had called upon his men to hold their hands. However, he had no intention of letting Jack off, and in his memory he made a note of the fact that there were additional blows coming to the lad.

The two men dropped their whips. One took Jack by the head and the other by the feet and they carried him back to his dungeon. There they left him, after first thrusting a pan of water and a small piece of bread into the cell.

Jack was brought back to himself by something cool upon his head. He stirred a bit and when at last he was able to sit up he became aware that his head was supported on a man's knee, while his temple was being bathed with cold water.

"How do you feel now?" demanded a voice, which Jack immediately recognized as that of the big Russian who had been with him on the first day he had been confined to the dungeon.

"Pretty weak," said Jack feebly. "I don't think I can undergo another such ordeal."

"A man never knows how much he can stand until put to the test," said the Russian, with a shrug of his shoulders that was imperceptible to Jack in the darkness.

"But how do you come to be back in here?" demanded Jack. "You were not here last night."

"No," said Boris. "But this morning, just after you had been so severely punished, I could keep quiet no longer and expressed myself to General Surgoff."

"With what result?" asked Jack.

Again the Russian shrugged, but Jack failed to see the gesture.

"The lash," he replied quietly. "Fifteen lashes; then the dungeon again."

Jack now got to his feet, though with some difficulty, and leaned on the Russian's arm.

"It's no use," he said, after pacing up and down the dark cell for some moments. "A person is a fool to stay here and put up with this sort of thing. Better death in the snow. To-morrow, when I am again led forth for my lashing, I shall make a break for liberty."

"It is impossible," said Boris. "You would be shot down before you had gone a dozen yards."

"That's where you are wrong," said Jack. "To General Surgoff, I am too valuable to be killed offhand. He would keep me alive until he is tired of seeing me suffer. After that, perhaps, he would order me shot; but until then no. If I can get anything like a start, perhaps I can reach one of the sleighs that always stand nearby. Then I can make a dash for liberty."

"By the Czar!" exclaimed Boris; "and perhaps after all you can reach the sleigh safely. I have a mind to go with you."

"You are the more likely to be shot down," said Jack. "The general, I fear, would have no scruples in ordering your death."

"Nevertheless," said Boris grimly, "with your permission I shall try it. Besides, if we do get away, two would be more handy than one."

"True," said Jack. "Now if we only had weapons."

"There may be a rifle or two left in the sleigh," said Boris hopefully.

"There may be," said Jack, "but we can't bank on that. There may not be."

"Then we shall have to go without weapons," said Boris finally.

Jack was deep in thought.

"I'm still weak from my beatings," he said at last, "but, if I am fortunate, I shall secure weapons for both of us. Not rifles, perhaps, but revolvers at least."

"How?" demanded Boris excitedly.

Jack smiled to himself in the darkness.

"I don't know exactly," he replied quietly, "though I have half an idea. Now we shall have to map out our plan of action."

"I'll let you do that," said Boris. "I am not much of a hand to figure; but when it comes to a fight you can count on me."

"You look as though you could give a good account of yourself," said Jack.

In the darkness he stretched forth his hand and felt Boris over carefully. The muscles swelled beneath the lad's touch and Jack knew that the Russian was indeed a powerful man.

"I'm no weakling," said the Russian modestly, "but for the matter of that neither are you. I have taken note of your build and I have thought to myself that, between us, we would be a hard pair to overcome."

Boris now extended a hand and felt the lad's arms and chest carefully. When he withdrew his hand he gave a grunt of satisfaction.

"You'll do," he said quietly. "Now as to your plan."

"Well," said Jack, "I have a half-formed plan. It will depend upon you to some extent what our chances of success are."

"You can count on me to the finish," said the Russian gravely.

"All right. Then what we shall do is this. When I am led forward to receive my lashing, you create a diversion of some kind. Give a yell or something, but make no dash toward the row of sleighs at that moment. It would prove fatal, for you would be shot down. However, make enough noise to attract attention your way. At that moment I'll jump the general and seize his revolvers — he most likely will be caught off his guard. Then I'll dash for the sleighs; and as soon as you see I have the general's weapons, you do the same. Whoever reaches there first will take the reins and be ready to whip up the horses the moment the other jumps in. That's all there is to the plan."

"It's not half bad," said the Russian, "and it promises a certain degree of success. So you are going to steal the general's revolvers, eh? I like that. And if he interferes with you, shoot him."

"Not if I can help it," said Jack. "I intend to come back here some day and attend to him with my hands."

"Ah, but he is too big for you there," protested Boris.

"Don't you believe it," said Jack dryly. "Take his guns away from him and give me fair play, and I'll promise I'll whip him good and properly."

"Perhaps," said the Russian, but he was plainly unconvinced. "But were I to make a wager, I would be forced to put my money on the general."

"I hope there will be no occasion for you to lose your money," said Jack, smiling.

"By the way," said the Russian after a pause, "how are your injuries? I can't see in the darkness, but I have no doubt the lash has left its mark."

"It has indeed," said Jack in reply. "My shoulders are bruised and bleeding. There are several welts across my face, and my legs and arms are very painful. But they feel better, now that I know I shall not stand still and receive more blows of the same kind."

"Well, you have put your mark on the general, anyhow," said Boris, his tone greatly pleased.

"So I have; but I have paid dearly for it," responded Jack.

It was Boris who finally put an end to the conversation.

"Take my advice," he said, "and get what rest you can to-day and to-night. To-morrow is near and there is no telling when you will sleep again. It is always well when a man has rested before he undertakes a desperate venture. He is in better condition."

"Your advice is good; I shall heed it," said Jack.

He lay down again in his corner and soon was asleep.

All day and all that night the two prisoners rested in the dungeon as well as they were able. It was impossible to sleep all the time, but they did no walking about; and when morning came they felt well and fit.

Each gulped down the water and bread that was thrust through the bars to them early in the morning; and each was on edge when the guard unlocked the heavy door and called upon them to emerge from their prison.

Boris stepped out as lively as a kitten, but Jack, to whom the work ahead seemed to be more serious, walked quietly, with head bent. Apparently taking the lad's attitude for one of fear, the Russian guard sneered audibly.

Boris caught the sound and looked up sharply. He opened his mouth to make a remark to the guard, but Jack, perceiving that Boris was about to cause trouble, raised a warning finger. Boris' mouth closed without saying a word, although Jack could see that he choked back the words at the tip of his tongue with an effort.

The lad smiled to himself.

"He'll be a pretty good partner," he muttered.

They followed the guard until they again stood in the presence of General Surgoff. The latter eyed them evilly as they approached, and motioned for Jack to step forward. The lad did so unhesitatingly. Boris would have followed, but the guards shoved him back among the crowd of other prisoners.

Jack looked quickly around as he stepped toward the Russian general. Some distance away, perhaps two hundred yards, he made out several sleighs, all ready to be put in use.

"If there were only one," he muttered; and he determined in that moment to try and frighten the other horses as he leaped into one sled.

He faced the Russian commander.

"And how do you feel this morning?" asked the general.

"Not very well, thank you, sir," returned Jack quietly.

"Feel like another little whipping will do you good, eh? Well, you shall have it."

"I just want to remark to you, general," said Jack quietly, "that you will rue the day you first laid the lash on me."

"What! You threaten me?" exclaimed General Surgoff. "You shall have an additional ten lashes this morning, whether you stand on your feet or fall fainting to the ground. Strip him, men."

The pair of Russians with their lashes stepped forward and would have laid hands on Jack; but Boris now decided that it was time for him to act.

He set up a sudden wild yell, that drew all eyes in his direction. It was the moment for which Jack has been waiting.

CHAPTER XXI.

ACROSS THE SNOW.

General Surgoff's head was turned toward where Boris and several Russian guards were struggling when Jack sprang upon his back like a cat. The general sent out a cry for help, but Jack cut it short as his hands closed about his opponent's throat.

Still retaining his grasp with his left hand, Jack's right dropped to the officer's belt. A revolver was quickly drawn and the lad stuffed it into his pocket. Then he seized the second revolver, shoved the Russian officer violently from him and dashed toward the sleighs.

There was a cry from behind and several rifles were brought to bear, but, even as Jack had expected, General Surgoff cried at the top of his voice:

"Take him alive! Death to the man who injures him!"

Jack shouted aloud as he continued to run toward the row of sleighs. Turning his head, he looked over his shoulder and saw that Boris too had eluded the men with whom he had been struggling and was running after him.

"Come on, Boris!" he cried, but Boris needed no urging and his feet seemed to fly over the ground. For a man of his size his speed was nothing short of remarkable.

Jack reached the row of sleighs well in advance of Boris. Of these conveyances there were four in all. Jack slapped the horses attached to three of the sleighs sharply and they dashed off. The fourth would have followed, but Jack leaped in, seized the reins and checked the animals. Then he waited calmly for Boris, who came rapidly toward him.

Jack still held one of General Surgoff's revolvers in his right hand, his left being sufficient to hold tight the reins. The lad saw one of the Russian guards stop in his tracks, throw his rifle to his shoulder and take aim at Boris.

Gripping the reins tighter with his left hand, the lad raised his revolver and fired quickly. The man who was aiming at Boris fell to the ground. Panting loudly, Boris now reached the sleigh and jumped in. Immediately Jack fired his revolver over his horses' heads and shook the reins over their backs.

"Giddap!" he shouted.

It is extremely doubtful if the animals understood Jack, but the reins slapping on their backs and the nearness of the revolver shot did the work. The animals dashed off with a jump.

Now from behind came the command Jack had been expecting. General Surgoff, seeing his victims about to make their escape from beneath his very eyes, shouted:

"Shoot!"

A volley of rifle bullets flew overhead and all about them. But none struck home and the horses continued their mad dash. A second and a third volley came with no better result.

"The fools!" muttered Jack. "Why don't they shoot one of the horses."

Apparently the guards had not thought of that, for no bullet came near the flying animals. Stooping low in the sleigh, Jack and Boris heard the whine of the bullets as they sped past. Several struck the back of the sleigh and were imbedded in the wooden seat.

But at last the flying horses drew the two fugitives out of range, whereupon Jack immediately checked their pace.

"No use wasting horseflesh unnecessarily," he said to Boris.

"Not a bit," was the rejoinder. "Say, that was a bit of quick work, wasn't it?"

"It was," agreed Jack.

"But what did you shoot at me for?" demanded the Russian.

"Shoot at you?" exclaimed Jack in surprise. "I didn't shoot at you."

"Why, you pointed your revolver right at me." "Oh, no I didn't," said Jack. "I was shooting over your head. One of the guards had drawn a bead on you with his rifle."

"And did you get him?"

"I did; else you wouldn't be here now."

"Thanks," said the big Russian. "I hope I am able to repay the debt some day."

"It was nothing," declared Jack. "Now, if we only knew where we were going, it would be all right."

"There is no place to go, so far as I know," said Boris. "All you wanted to do when you started, if you will remember, was to get away where there would be no more lashings. We are away now, so what more can you ask?"

"You mean that we will just wander around until we die of cold or starvation?" asked Jack.

"Exactly."

"Well, we won't," said Jack. "We'll go along with some definite object in view. Now, which way would you take the railroad to be?"

Boris swung an arm in a southerly direction.

"Off there—some place," he said.

"Good; then we'll head that way," and Jack swung the horses in the direction indicated.

"But there is no chance of reaching the railroad," protested Boris.

"There is always a chance," said Jack calmly. "Always a fighting chance so long as one has breath in his body. It is better to be moving toward a definite objective than to lie idle and wait for death."

"Well, I guess you are right there," said Boris. "But after we reach the railroad—if we do reach it—then what? If we are picked up we will probably be sent right back where we came from."

"We won't cross that bridge until we come to it," returned Jack quietly. "Our first consideration is to reach the railroad."

"If we could be so fortunate as to strike a road," said Boris, "we might have a chance; but to go driving through the snow like this, blindly, we have no hope of getting there."

"Do you suppose these horses have been over the road often enough to pick it out themselves?" asked Jack.

"I don't know; you might try them."

Jack gave the animals their head. Immediately they slowed down, and then the off horse began to pull toward the right. After some resistance the other followed him.

"He's going some place," said Jack hopefully.

"And we are going along," replied Boris with a grim attempt at humor.

Half a mile ahead, having pulled the sleigh over steep piles of drifted snow, the horses again headed southward. The going was much easier. The ground ahead now showed signs of recent travel.

"By Jove! They have picked the trail," declared Jack.

"So they have," said Boris. "Do you know, I am beginning to have hopes that we shall reach the railroad."

"Of course we shall," said Jack confidently. "It may be hard work, but we shall reach there."

"And then?" demanded Boris.

Again Jack shrugged his shoulders.

"Who knows?" he muttered and gave his undivided attention to the road that stretched out ahead.

All day they drove slowly along, for they did not wish to tire the horses more than was necessary. It was bitterly cold, but the two travelers had been fortunate enough to find heavy rugs in the sleigh, and these kept them quite comfortable. Also Jack had come upon one pair of gloves. These had to do for both, so the one kept his ungloved hands beneath the robes while the other did the driving.

It grew dusk.

Jack, glancing back down the road, saw a moving object coming after them. It looked like a dog and the lad called Boris' attention to the form loping along behind them, apparently content to remain at the same relative distance.

Boris took one look at the following form and cried out:

"A wolf!"

"Wolf!" cried Jack. "I thought it was a dog. Oh, well, no matter. We can certainly take care of a lone wolf."

"So we can," said Boris dryly. "The trouble is that by an hour after dark it won't be a lone wolf. There will be wolves by the score upon our track."

"But can't we outrun them?" asked Jack fearfully.

"We might, if our horses were fresh. But you must remember we have traveled all day."

"Then we shall have to fight," declared Jack quietly.

"Of course," said Boris briefly. "But with our hands we can do little."

Jack produced Surgoff's revolvers and passed one of them to Boris.

"These will help a little," he said.

"A little, but not much," said Boris with a shake of his head. "A few wolves shot down and there will still be more."

He glanced over his shoulder again.

"Look!" he exclaimed. "There is another!"

Jack looked back and his heart beat more fast as he saw that the first loping gray figure had been joined by a second and that they came forward rapidly.

"There will be more of them directly," said Boris calmly.

"Well, we have wasted time enough," declared Jack at this point. "Before the pack assembles, I believe it would be well for us to whip up and put as much distance between us and the wolves as possible."

"We won't be able to put much," said Boris pessimistically. "The faster we go the faster they will go, until the pack has closed in, and then they will come to the attack."

"Can you shoot?" asked Jack suddenly.

"Like a flash," was the reply. "I can hit anything that can be hit. Why?"

"Then you do the shooting and I'll do the driving," said Jack. "Here, you take both these guns. Give me the reins and the whip."

The exchange was made, and Jack touched the backs of the horses lightly with the whip.

"If we were only near to a human habitation of some kind," he muttered to Boris.

"Well, we may and we may not be," was the reply. "But these fellows will follow us right to the edge of the city. It's been a hard winter and they are hungry. Hear them howl?"

It was a blood-curdling sound that Jack heard then. It sent a shiver down his spine.

"It's the call of the pack," said Boris briefly. "They'll be down on us in a moment. See, in the darkness back there now there are fully a score."

For answer Jack got up to his feet and the long whip whistled through the air and over the horses' necks. But the animals, too, had caught the scent of the wolves, and they needed no urging. They dashed forward. And at that moment Boris, glancing back, shouted:

"Here they come!"

CHAPTER XXII.

THE BATTLE WITH THE WOLVES.

The pack came forward with a rush. Great, long, gaunt figures, they covered the ground with remarkable speed. Each bound brought them closer to the swift-flying sleigh in spite of the best efforts the tired horses could put forth; and they were putting forth their best, for they were in even greater fear than the human load they bore.

Now the first wolf reached the back of the sleigh and launched itself in a desperate leap. His forefeet found their mark, but he had not gauged the distance accurately and he slipped back; but he tried again. The second time the leap was more true and he clung to the back of the sleigh and attempted to pull himself up.

It was that moment that Boris fired. The ball sped true and the first wolf went tumbling back into the road.

Immediately the others of the pack set upon him and tore him to pieces with their sharp teeth; then they dashed forward again.

But the second attack seemed to have been carefully thought out. While several of the larger wolves leaped for the back of the sleigh, others of the pack darted by the sleigh on either side and sprang upon the horses. Jack turned his whip from the backs of the horses and lashed out at the wolves. Some he hit and some he missed; but he swung the long whip with great violence and for the moment the attack was beaten off. In the rear, Boris had also been successful a second time.

Thus they gained a breathing space and Boris called out:

"I have only two shots left!"

"Then it looks as though we were done for," said Jack quietly, as he continued to ply the whip and the horses sped on.

A hundred yards ahead, the road turned sharply and the panic-stricken horses dashed madly around it. The wolf-pack was now some distance back, for they had stopped over another fallen comrade.

Suddenly Jack let out a cry of joy. Not a hundred yards ahead was a small building of some kind—in the darkness the lad could not make out just what—but it was a refuge.

Quickly he imparted the good news to Boris and cried:

"Drop off and run for the door as we go by."

The lad threw the reins upon the horses' backs and climbed to the back of the sleigh, as did Boris. Then, just as the sleigh went flying past the low building, they dropped to the ground.

Both went sprawling, but they were up quickly and dashing toward the door of the little hut, as it now appeared to be. From behind, the wolf-pack, seeing their prey so near, leaped forward with renewed energy.

"Open the door quick!" shouted Jack.

Boris laid hold of the knob, turned it and pushed vigorously. The door opened and Boris stepped back to let Jack pass in first. The lad hesitated a brief moment and then sprang inside. Boris would have followed, but at that moment three gray figures launched themselves through the air.

Boris' revolver spoke twice—his two last cartridges were now gone—and two of the enemy fell to the ground; but the leap of the third wolf—the largest of the pack—carried him to Boris' shoulder.

The Russian was borne to the ground.

He was up in a minute with a terrible cry, and seizing the wolf in both his great hands, he plucked him from him; then, turning, he threw the animal squarely into the pack as it dashed upon him.

The pack gave back and Boris took advantage of that moment to spring within the hut and slam shut the door; even as the wolves, recovering, leaped against it.

Inside the two fugitives hurriedly barred the door and sank to the floor, tired out from their exertions.

"Safe!" panted Jack at last, getting to his feet.

"I guess so," returned Boris. "They can't get in here unless there is a window open. Look around quickly."

They explored the hut in the semi-darkness — a faint light reflected from the snow without permitting them to see. Examining the window through which the light came Jack found it covered by glass.

"Guess they won't try that way," he said.

"You never can tell," replied Boris with a shake of his head. "If they are really desperate and hungry, they may try to spring through. The first would break the glass and the others would have no trouble getting in."

"Well, it's the only window in the place; we should be able to guard it," said Jack.

He looked about the floor and at last picked up a big log that lay before the old fireplace. It was heavy, but the lad wielded it without difficulty.

"We should be able to hold them off with this," he said.

The Russian looked at the weapon and nodded.

"By the Czar!" he exclaimed. "I had no idea you could handle that weight so easily."

"As I told you before, I am no weakling," replied Jack quietly. "We shall take turns at the door. I suppose the pack will draw off with the coming of day?"

"It depends," said Boris, "upon how close we happen to be to other human beings. If we are close to the railroad, where men pass frequently, the pack will probably draw off at daylight. If not, we shall have to stand a siege."

At that moment there was a sound of crashing glass and both looked toward the window just in time to see a huge grey shape come flying through and alight upon its feet on the floor.

Jack raised his log and would have brought it down on the animal's head, but Boris cried:

"Guard the window! I'll take care of this one."

130

Jack leaped to obey and arrived just in time to bring the log crashing down on another head as it showed itself. While Boris struggled with the wolf inside, the lad disposed of four of the enemy.

Boris and the wolf that had succeeded in gaining an entrance sprang toward each other at the same moment. Both were wounded already, Boris with a bite in the shoulder from the animal he had encountered before entering the hut, and the wolf from a cut inflicted by the ragged pieces of glass as he passed through the window.

Boris presented his side as the wolf dodged and stepped slightly aside. The animal's teeth nipped the Russian's clothes, but failed to reach the flesh. Before the beast could recover, Boris had seized him by the throat with both hands.

A mighty grip, this, and the wolf struggled in vain, scratching and wriggling as it was lifted clear off the floor. Holding him at arm's length, Boris continued to shut off the beast's wind. The wolf gurgled once, twice and then became limp in Boris' hands.

But Boris was wary. He had no mind to allow himself to be tricked, knowing well that a wolf, sometimes when cornered, resorted to all sorts of subterfuges. Boris held his grip for several minutes; then flung the wolf's body from him.

"I guess that settles you," he said quietly.

He approached the window to lend Jack a helping hand if necessary; but the enemy, having lost four of their number there, hung back.

"I don't think they will try it again for a while," said Jack calmly.

"You can't tell," returned Boris. "Sometimes they never give up. Now you keep guard here and I'll see if I can't start a fire. We would be safer then."

Jack nodded and Boris turned away. A few moments later Jack heard him give a grunt of satisfaction.

"Find anything?" the lad called.

"Plenty to start a fire," was the response. "Wood, husks and matches. I'll have a fire going in this fireplace in a few moments. Then we shall be safe."

The big Russian was as good as his word, and a few minutes later a cheerful blaze filled the fireplace.

"Now," said the Russian, "I wonder if I couldn't scare up a little food?"

He rummaged about in the drawers of a table at the far end of the room and presently returned to the fireplace carrying a piece of cold meat.

"Don't know what it is, but it will do," was his comment. "I'm too hungry to be very particular."

"So am I," Jack agreed.

The Russian produced a long knife from one of the drawers and cut the piece of meat in two, handing half to Jack. They devoured it ravenously.

"Not so bad," said Jack, smacking his lips when the last piece had disappeared down his throat. "Tastes funny, though. What do you suppose it was?"

"Horse," was the brief reply.

Jack gulped and swallowed several times before he could force himself to reply:

"Wha—what's that?"

"Horse," repeated Boris. "Didn't you ever eat horse before?"

"N-n-no, I guess not," replied Jack, feeling somewhat sick at his stomach.

"It's good," said Boris. "Next to a piece of beef, give me a good piece of horseflesh. Why," noting the queer expression on Jack's face, "you don't mean to tell me you don't like it?"

"I can't say that I am fond of it," replied the lad truthfully.

"But——" began Boris.

Jack jumped to his feet.

"Please don't talk about it any more," he said with a sickly smile. "If I have eaten a piece of horse, all right. But I don't want to be told about it."

"Ho! ho!" laughed Boris. "Now what do you think of that! Here is a brave young man turning sick just because he has swallowed a piece of horse. Ho! ho!"

He laughed long and loudly.

"Won't you please keep quiet?" asked Jack, getting sicker every minute. "Horse! Ugh!"

Realizing that the lad really and truly didn't like such talk, the Russian desisted. He arose and walked to the window. Without, but some distance from the hut now that the fire was blazing freely in the open place, stood the gaunt, gray wolves. Boris called Jack to him.

"They'll stay there as long as this fire is kept burning," he explained. "But there is no need for both of us to stand guard. One can watch and keep the fire going and the other can sleep. We'll divide the night into four-hour watches. You lie down on the pallet there in the corner. I'll stand the first watch."

Jack did as Boris suggested and was soon asleep; and all through the long night, inside the hut one stood guard as the other slept — and the break of day did not come any too suddenly.

CHAPTER XXIII.

CAPTURED BY NEW ENEMIES.

Dawn came early in Boris' second watch. The wolves still maintained their vigil without. The Russian kept the fire blazing brightly. He determined to let Jack sleep an hour longer.

But this was not to be.

Glancing from the window, Boris saw the wolves suddenly begin to move away. It was strange and the Russian was unable to account for it. But he was not long making out the cause of the trouble.

Came the sound of footsteps without—not a sound made by a single man, but rather by a large body of men. Boris became instantly apprehensive, and tip-toeing across the room, he aroused Jack quietly. As the lad opened his eyes the Russian laid a warning finger to his lips:

"Sh-h-sh," he said softly.

"What's the matter now?" demanded Jack. "Wolves?"

Boris shook his head.

"Surgoff?" whispered Jack.

"Can't tell yet," was the reply. "There are men outside. Perhaps they will pass by without looking in."

"No such luck, with those dead wolves out there," said Jack.

The lad was right. Suddenly there came a voice from without, raised in surprise.

"Ho! There must be men within the hut—dead or alive. See the dead wolves? There must have been a battle. We shall go in."

The footsteps approached the door. A moment later there was a loud knock.

"Shall we open the door?" whispered Jack.

"May as well," replied Boris. "If we don't, they will break the door in."

Came a second heavy knock on the door and a voice called:

"Is there any one there?"

"One moment and I shall unbar the door," Boris called back.

The door opened at last, three men, cloaked in the uniform of Russian officers, strode in. They eyed Jack and Boris keenly.

"What are you doing here?" demanded one, evidently the commander.

"We took shelter here from the wolves," replied Boris guardedly, for, if possible, he did not wish to tell the officers they had recently come from the direction of the Siberian prison camp.

"Where from?" asked the officer.

"From the north," was the reply.

"Where are your horses and sleigh?"

Boris shrugged his shoulders.

"Probably devoured by wolves by this time, your excellency," he returned. "When we leaped out the horses were still running and the wolves after them."

"Are you from the prison camp?" demanded the officer suddenly.

The question came so suddenly that, although Boris had been expecting it, it caught him off his guard. His face turned red as he stammered:

"Why—why, n-no, your excellency."

"That," said the officer, who had not been fooled, "is an untruth. When did you escape?"

"Yesterday," replied Boris in a dull voice, for it was evident to him that it was only a question of time until he would be back in the dungeon.

"Why?"

"Because we were cruelly treated, your excellency," said Jack, stepping forward and taking a hand in the conversation.

"Surely you don't expect ladylike treatment here in Siberia?" suggested the officer with a grin.

135

"Hardly, sir," returned Jack. "But this is no treatment for a British officer, and when his Majesty learns of it, you may make sure that the Czar will take some drastic action, sir."

"Oho! so you know the Czar, eh?"

The Russian smiled sneeringly.

"Yes, I know the Czar," returned Jack quietly; "and if you are wise, you will be careful of your actions."

The lad's statement seemed, for some reason, to impress the officer. He dropped his tone of banter and said:

"Well, we shall see about your case. I shall conduct you back to General Surgoff myself. First, however, I have other business. I am sent to meet General Burgoff, who is coming to Siberia on some mysterious mission. We will move toward the railroad. In the meantime, you are both my prisoners."

The officer signaled them to leave the hut, which they did. Outside they found a large body of men in sleighs, in one of which there was room for two more men. The officer motioned Jack and Boris in, and after instructing his men to see that they were carefully guarded, the party drove off.

It was shortly after noon that they came in sight of the railroad, and Jack made out the same station where the train had stopped when he had entered his first fight in Siberia. The party rode up to the station and alighted. All entered the station, where the officer approached the operator.

"Special train will be here in half an hour, sir," replied the operator in reply to the officer's question. "You are in good time, sir."

"Very well," said the officer.

He sat down to wait.

It was less than half an hour later that a distant rumble gave notice that the train was approaching. A few moments later it drew up at the station. The Russian officer uttered an exclamation of astonishment as troops began to pour from the twenty cars.

"By the Czar!" he exclaimed. "I wonder why General Burgoff comes in such force? I had expected that he would come practically alone. Here he must have five thousand men!"

Nevertheless he advanced to meet the Russian commander without delay.

General Burgoff descended from his car with a firm step and haughty mien. He did not pay much attention to the officer who came forward to greet him, other than to return his salute and say a few words. He spoke to one of his own officers.

"Have the men on the march immediately," he said sharply.

The latter saluted and moved away.

The general entered the station and by his side walked Frank, come to Siberia to find his friend and chum. And no sooner had Frank entered the station that his eyes rested upon Jack.

"Jack!" he cried and dashed forward.

Jack turned quickly in utter amazement at the sound of his chum's voice.

"Frank!" he cried joyfully, and half rose, only to be pushed down again by one of the soldiers who guarded him.

Frank turned upon the soldier and cried:

"Let him alone."

At this moment the Russian officer who had captured Jack and Boris came up.

"Look here," he said to Frank. "These men are my prisoners and neither you nor any one else can interfere with them."

"Is that so?" shouted Frank, losing his temper. "Well, I'll — —"

A firm hand was laid on the lad's arm and he looked into the face of General Burgoff; the general's face wore a peculiar smile.

"Silence, if you please," said the general. "I shall attend to this matter myself."

Frank drew back a trifle as General Burgoff turned toward the officer who accosted Frank.

"You, sir," said the general sternly, "are hereby relieved of the custody of your prisoners. I shall accept the responsibility; and in the future when you address any one at all, let it be in more of a gentlemanly manner."

The officer flushed at this rebuke.

"But sir," he protested, "I must make my report to General Surgoff, sir. He is in command in Siberia and he will not like your having taken my prisoners from me."

"Now don't let that worry you, colonel. You need report to General Surgoff no more except when I tell you to."

The colonel bowed.

"I do not know your authority, sir," he said, "but I must yield to you as my superior officer. The prisoners are yours, sir; but I would add, if you will permit me, that they have escaped from General Surgoff and that he would probably be glad of their return."

"Very well," said the general. "I am going to pay my respects to General Surgoff. You may consider yourself on my staff for the present. Now present my compliments to Colonel Luskowith and tell him to march immediately."

The colonel bowed and departed. General Burgoff advanced to Jack's side.

"So!" he exclaimed, "the young Englishman whom I sentenced to Siberia, eh?"

"The same," said Jack briefly.

"I have come," continued the general, "to tell you that I have discovered my grievous error, to release you and to ask your pardon."

Jack was on his feet instantly.

"Say no more about it, sir," he exclaimed. "You were greatly worried and overwrought at the time, sir. Any man will make a mistake, sir."

The general looked at the lad keenly and then extended his hand. Jack grasped it. Then the general turned to Boris.

"And your fellow prisoner?" he asked.

"Boris," said Jack. "He has aided me greatly in making my escape."

"Then, for that reason, if for no other," said General Burgoff, "I shall not question the reason of his imprisonment. He is free."

The general motioned the soldiers who guarded the two to stand aside.

"And now," he added, "tell me how you have been treated. Have you any complaint to make?"

Jack's lips set sternly.

"Do not think I am whining, sir," he said, "when I say that the treatment accorded prisoners by General Surgoff and his underlings is barbarous."

"Tell me," said the general.

Jack told of his own treatment and that of other prisoners as he had witnessed it. General Burgoff's face turned red as the lad progressed, and when he had concluded, he said:

"Yes, I shall pay my respects to General Surgoff, and at the Czar's command. So that is the way prisoners are treated in Siberia, eh?"

"General," said Jack, "I have a favor to ask."

"Name it; it is granted," was the reply.

"Then, sir, in respect to General Surgoff, will you not follow my plan?" and the lad outlined an idea that had come into his head.

When Jack stopped talking, General Burgoff clapped his hands and exclaimed:

"Good! Good! It shall be done! Come, gentlemen, we shall move at once. I shall indeed be glad to see my dear General Surgoff!"

CHAPTER XXIV.

A SEVERE REPRIMAND.

General Surgoff had word of General Burgoff's approach long before the long line of troops appeared in sight. The former immediately made preparations to receive him.

It was an hour after the first troops came within view of the prison camp that General Burgoff and General Surgoff saluted each other. Then the latter extended his hand, but General Burgoff appeared not to see it.

Said the Siberian commander:

"If you will come to my quarters, sir, I shall be pleased to make you at home."

"Thank you, sir," was the reply, "but first I would deliver to you two prisoners whom I have picked up."

He summoned his orderly. The latter went away and returned a few moments later with Jack and Boris, surrounded by a file of soldiers. At sight of them, General Surgoff's eyes lighted up.

"Ah!" he exclaimed. "They escaped from here very recently, General Burgoff. I am indeed glad to have them back again, especially the young one. I shall teach him a lesson that he shall not forget if he lives to be a hundred; and with your permission, sir, I shall do it now."

"I shall be glad to see the form of punishment you use in Siberia," was the other's reply.

Immediately the Siberian commander summoned two men, who it appeared were his official "lashers." They came forward with their long whips, and cruel smiles on their features. General Surgoff indicated Jack with a gesture of his right arm.

"Strip him and give him thirty hard lashes!" he ordered.

The men sprang forward and laid hands on the lad, who submitted without a murmur. General Surgoff eyed him with an evil smile.

"So!" he exclaimed. "I have you back, eh? Well, before I am through with you, you will wish you had died in the snow. Hurry, men!"

The two men now stepped back and raised their whips. But before the first blow could be struck, General Burgoff sprang forward.

"Stop!" he commanded in a harsh voice.

Somewhat bewildered the men dropped their whips.

General Surgoff turned upon General Burgoff angrily.

"What do you mean, sir?" he demanded.

"I mean that things like this shall come to an end," declared the other. "There will be no more of this brutality in Siberia, when it is in my power to stop it."

"In your power, sir?" questioned General Surgoff. "You forget, sir, I am in command here. The punishment shall proceed. Apply the lash, men!"

"One moment," said General Burgoff quietly, raising a hand.

Again the men dropped the whips they had raised. General Burgoff turned to the Siberian commander.

"I have allowed this matter to proceed thus far," he said, "because I desired to see how you conducted matters here. I have seen enough. And besides having seen, I have heard. Your sword, sir!"

General Surgoff staggered back in utmost amazement.

"Wha—what's that?" he demanded, hardly believing the senses of his own ears.

"Your sword, and at once," said General Burgoff. "You may consider yourself under arrest, sir."

A slow smile flitted over the other's face, now that he was sure he had understood.

"You forget, sir," he replied, "that I am in command here. I, sir, in turn, demand your sword for having interfered with your superior officer."

General Burgoff laughed aloud.

"Surely," he said, "you don't think I would make such a demand without some assurance that I could enforce my orders. Come, sir, your sword, and quickly."

"And by whose command do you act?" asked General Surgoff, somewhat uneasily.

"At the command of the Czar!"

General Surgoff again staggered.

"But—but——" he began.

"Silence," interrupted General Burgoff. He drew a piece of paper from his pocket and passed it to the other. "By this," he said, "I am empowered to relieve you of your command in Siberia and I have full authority to act in your place."

General Surgoff read the paper and his eyes flashed dangerously. Suddenly he tore the paper into little bits and turned upon the other defiantly.

"There is your authority," he said, and threw the fragments of paper to the wind. "You are powerless to touch me now."

Again General Burgoff smiled.

"You are a fool," he said pleasantly. "Why do you think I came here at the head of five thousand men? Either you will give me your sword this moment as a sign that you recognize my authority, or I shall put you and your entire command under arrest, if I have to shoot half of them down to do so."

"But sir," protested the other, "surely you will not humiliate me in the sight of my men."

"You cannot be humiliated, sir," was the reply. "You are too low for that. It gives me pleasure, sir, to tell you that you are a coward and a cur."

General Surgoff's hand dropped to his sword belt.

"No man can call me that," he said, "and live."

"But I do," declared his successor. "I call you that and I shall live to see you brought before the Czar. Now sir, for the last time, your sword."

Slowly General Surgoff drew his sword and seemed on the point of passing it to the officer who had relieved him of his command. But suddenly he raised it before him and sprang forward with a cry.

General Burgoff was taken completely off his guard. Not so Jack. He had been eyeing Surgoff closely and had half expected some such move. Therefore, at the moment the man leaped forward, so did Jack.

With his right hand the lad struck the officer's arm and then closed with him. With a sudden movement he seized the arm that held the sword and he twisted it sharply. The sword went flying through the air and struck ten yards away, while the Russian sought in vain to free himself from the lad's clutch.

At length, believing he had the man powerless, Jack released his hold and stepped back.

With a sudden movement the infuriated officer whipped out a revolver and aiming it directly at the lad, pressed the trigger.

Jack had seen the movement, but he was so surprised that he seemed to be rooted to the spot. He was unable to move.

But there had been another close witness of the struggle and the quick action of this watcher alone saved Jack's life.

Frank had sprung suddenly forward and succeeded in knocking up the Russian's arm at the very moment his finger tightened on the trigger.

Jack therefore emerged from the cloud of smoke unharmed.

Now Frank had grappled with the officer and was seeking to wrest the revolver from his hand. But the lad was no match for the big Russian. Jack sprang forward just in time to lend a helping hand and General Surgoff was subdued without much trouble.

"Now," said General Burgoff to the deposed officer, "I shall have the pleasure of informing the Czar that you attempted to assassinate me. Do you realize what that will mean?"

General Surgoff made no reply, though he glared at the other angrily.

"By the way, General," said Jack, stepping forward at that moment, "you haven't forgotten the promise you made me, have you?"

General Burgoff smiled.

"No danger," he returned. "I shall be an interested witness."

He turned again to General Surgoff. "Surgoff," he said, "did you ever hear of men fighting with their fists?"

"Yes," was the answer, in a snarling voice. "I have had some such experience myself. I took boxing lessons under an English instructor. Why do you ask?"

"Because," was the reply, "this young British officer here," and he indicated Jack with a motion of his head, "tells me that he has a score to settle with you and that he would be glad to settle it by the use of his fists. If you are proficient in that art of fighting, so much the better. You may possibly save yourself a severe thrashing."

"And you mean that you are going to consent to such a thing?" demanded the other.

"I am; most decidedly. Even now I can see the marks of the lash on this lad's face. Certainly he is entitled to payment; and I intend to see that he gets it. If you refuse to fight, I shall have you lashed myself."

General Surgoff eyed Jack keenly. The lad, though not as tall and broad as the officer, still was husky enough to give the general an idea that he would not be easily conquered. Besides, through long residence in Great Britain in his younger days, the officer had come to hold a great respect for the Englishman when it came to the use of fists. Still, compared with himself, Jack seemed small. Surgoff became possessed of the idea that he could overcome him.

"I'll fight him," he said in answer to General Burgoff's last remark. "But I want to tell him now that he will be sorry he ever crossed my path." Jack smiled pleasantly.

"Because of the chance that I shall have at you now," he said, "I am glad that I encountered you. You may believe me, for every lash of the whip you have given me, you shall pay now. I will not let you off too easily."

"You boast," said the other. "It is unwise. Before I am through with you you will be crying another tune."

"Perhaps," said Jack quietly. "Well, General," turning to General Burgoff, "whenever you say, sir."

"It may as well be now," was the reply. "Are you ready, Surgoff?"

"Yes."

He stripped off his outer garments and rolled up his sleeves. Jack did likewise. Frank stepped forward.

"If you please, sir?" he said. "I would like to run this thing. I know more of boxing than you, sir."

The general nodded his permission.

"Proceed," he said.

CHAPTER XXV.

THE FIGHT.

Frank stepped forward and called both combatants to him.

"The fight will start when I give the word," he said. "There will be no rounds. You will keep fighting until one of you can fight no more. My job shall be to see that you, Surgoff, do not resort to unfair methods. I assure you that if you do, I shall tap you over the head with my revolver. Now you both understand, do you?"

Jack nodded.

"Yes," said Surgoff surlily.

"All right. Then go."

Surgoff sprang forward with a cry, apparently bent on disposing of his opponent with a single blow. In spite of the fact that he knew well the power of the Englishman when it came to fists, he threw caution to the winds. It was perfectly plain that he considered himself more than a match for Jack.

Jack avoided the rush by sidestepping neatly and as the Russian was carried by by the force of his rush, Jack planted a heavy blow solidly above the right ear. The big Russian went reeling. Jack leaped lightly forward and before his opponent could recover himself, he had stepped around him and drove a left to the jaw.

The Russian covered as best he could and gave ground. Jack followed him closely, and succeeded in driving three blows under the other's guard. Then the Russian rushed into a clinch.

He clung to the lad tenaciously and it was only by a violent effort that Jack succeeded in hurling him away. Surgoff went sprawling on the ground. Jack stepped back and waited for his fallen foe to rise.

"I don't want to end this too quickly," he said between set teeth.

Surgoff staggered to his feet and raised his guard, waiting for the lad to come to him. Apparently he had had enough of rushing tactics and had determined to put up a defensive battle. Nothing loath, Jack advanced, treading lightly on his toes.

The lad feinted sharply with his left for the head, and drove his right fist squarely to the pit of the Russian's stomach. Surgoff doubled up like a jack-knife and fell forward to the ground, where he rolled and tumbled about for the space of several minutes. Again Jack stood by quietly, waiting for him to rise.

No sooner was the man on his feet again that Jack rushed forward. Again he feinted with his left—this time for the stomach—and as the Russian lowered his guard to ward off the blow, Jack's right fist caught him on the nose. Jack had drawn first blood.

Now Jack stood off at long range and peppered his opponent beautifully, much to the delight of the large crowd of officers and men that had gathered about, and was increasing at every moment, as word of the encounter was passed along.

In vain did the Russian try to ward off the sledge-hammer blows. Jack was not to be denied; and there was no pity in the lad's heart, for he remembered his own lashings and the lashings of others, men, women and children. He had determined to pay Surgoff in full.

Again Surgoff rushed into a clinch. Jack felt the man's hands close about his throat, and the Russian had a powerful grip. But both of Jack's hands were free, and he loosened the other's hold by driving a straight right to the stomach. For a third time the Russian general rolled on the ground.

Jack smiled grimly as he waited for the man to regain his feet.

"Now," he said, when Surgoff again faced him, "we'll count off twenty good blows and then call it square."

"Smack!"

His right fist caught his opponent upon the sore nose.

"Smack! Smack!"

Right and left crashed against Surgoff's jaws.

147

"Smack!"

Another to the sore nose.

And so it continued, Jack counting the blows aloud.

"Sixteen," he said quietly, as he drove an extra-vicious left jolt to the man's swollen right eye.

"Seventeen!" and he closed the right optic with his right.

"Eighteen!" and Surgoff staggered weakly from the effect of a blow to the nose.

"Nineteen!" cried Jack, as he brought the man forward with an extra-violent blow to the stomach.

Then, the man absolutely at his mercy. Jack dropped his right arm low and swung from the shoulder. Straight and true went the blow and caught Surgoff squarely upon the point of the chin.

"Twenty!" said Jack quietly.

He turned toward where Frank was standing; and thus did not see Surgoff sink weakly to one knee and then tumble to the ground face downward.

"Well, I've evened up my score," said Jack to General Burgoff.

"And you have done it handsomely," was the reply. "By the Czar! this fighting with fists must be a great game. I had no idea a man could do a foe such injury."

"Well, I suppose I could have done it a bit quicker," said Jack. "But I didn't want to put him out too suddenly. It would have been too merciful, and I cannot see that a man like him is entitled to mercy. Still, I flatter myself I did an artistic job."

"You did," agreed the general.

Jack now glanced toward his fallen foe, who was returning to consciousness.

Slowly Surgoff raised himself upon his elbow; then struggled to his knees and at last to his feet. Not a hand was extended to help him. Seeing Jack

148

standing some distance away, eyeing him, Surgoff raised a fist and shook it at the lad as hard as his feebleness would permit.

"You shall pay for this," he exclaimed in a hoarse voice. "You shall answer to me some day. If I ever get you in my power, you will rue this day's work."

Jack smiled scornfully.

"I shall make it a point never to fall into your power," he said quietly.

He turned his back upon the Russian.

Now General Burgoff advanced and glared at the vanquished Russian officer.

"Go to your quarters at once, sir!" he commanded. "You are under arrest."

Without a word, General Surgoff turned on his heel and made his way slowly to his own quarters.

"What are you going to do with him, sir?" asked Jack.

"Take him before the Czar," was the reply.

"But why trouble His Majesty?" said Jack. "Surely he has been punished enough. Why not let him go?"

"By the Czar!" exclaimed General Burgoff again. "So you are so forgiving, eh? Now, were I in your place, I could wish nothing better than to see him hanged."

"I don't want to see any man hanged, sir," returned Jack decidedly.

"Well, that's the difference between an Englishman and a Russian," said the general. "However, you are the fellow who has suffered. I shall do as you suggest."

"Then, sir, simply deprive him of his rank and let him go."

The general threw wide his arms.

"It shall be done," he said.

He summoned his orderly.

"Have General Surgoff brought back here," he commanded.

The orderly saluted and moved away. He was back a few moments later followed by the deposed commander.

"And what do you want with me now?" demanded the latter somewhat aggressively.

"If I were you," returned General Burgoff quietly, "I would adopt another tone. That kind of talk will do you no good and I am likely to change my mind regarding what disposition I shall make of you."

"Influenced by this Englishman, perhaps," sneered General Surgoff, with a malevolent look at Jack.

"Hardly," was the grim reply. "Surgoff, I have decided that it is unnecessary to take you before the Czar. I shall attend to your case myself."

"You mean that I shall be put to death?" exclaimed the other. "Certainly you dare not shoulder such a responsibility."

"I dare anything," was the reply. "But such is not my intention. No; I shall simply turn your command over to your immediately subordinate and allow you to go free, first commanding that you leave Siberia immediately."

For a moment it seemed that General Surgoff could not believe he had heard aright. Then he stepped toward General Burgoff and said brokenly:

"I thank you, sir. I shall go to the front and seek to enlist in the ranks. Perhaps it is not too late for me to serve Russia well."

"Do," replied General Burgoff in a more kindly voice. "But do not thank me for this chance. Thank this young Englishman here."

General Surgoff stared at Jack in the utmost surprise. Plainly such cases of forgiveness were beyond his comprehension.

"I bear you no ill will," said Jack quietly.

"But I do you," growled the deposed officer. "I shall accept this chance, sir," turning to the general again, "but I will thank no one but you. And one more word," again turning to Jack, "if ever I am fortunate enough to lay hands on you, I shall make you pay."

Jack shrugged his shoulders.

"Oh, all right, if that's the way you feel about it," he said with a slight smile.

General Surgoff saluted General Burgoff stiffly; turned on his heel and marched away.

"You see," said the latter to Jack. "You see what forgiveness means to a man like Surgoff."

"Oh, well," said Jack, "at least I have kept my own conscience clear. That is something."

General Burgoff eyed the lad keenly for some moments, considering this remark. At last he turned away; and he also shrugged his shoulders; and he said:

"You are right, my lad. That is something!"

CHAPTER XXVI.

JACK IN THE TOILS.

Petrograd again.

It was evening five days after Frank and Jack had returned to the Russian capital from Siberia. Since their arrival they had made several trips of inspection to the D-17, but upon their last visit this same day they learned that it would be another week before the submarine was ready to take to sea again.

The lads had passed the long five days in various ways. They had received the thanks of the Czar for the part they had played in exposing Count Blowinski and His Majesty had commissioned them honorary lieutenants in the Russian army.

Of days they had strolled about the city taking in the sights of interest; of nights they had taken in the theaters—for there was still amusement to be found in Petrograd—a few of the most popular restaurants and other places where crowds congregated.

As the two lads walked along the street this particular evening they were discussing the D-17 and the fact that they were soon to put to sea again.

"I'll be glad to get back in British waters again," said Jack.

"So will I," agreed Frank, "but there is no sign that when we leave here we shall go straight home."

"Where else would we go?"

"I don't know. But you must remember Lord Hastings has begun to keep his plans more to himself than he used to do. In fact, he told us so. We are just as likely to head for the Dardanelles or South Africa, for all we know."

"Well, that's so, too," said Jack. "However, I have one of those things you call—that you call—By Jove! I can't think of the word. Premonitions, I mean."

"The word you want," said Frank, "is hunch."

"That's it," cried Jack. "A hunch. I have a hunch that it will not be long before we are back in England."

"Well, I won't object to that."

"I will be glad," said Jack, "when the time comes when we can go ashore and stay — when the war will be a thing of the past."

"I am afraid that is a long ways off."

"It does seem so. And still when peace does come, it probably will come suddenly."

At this point in the conversation Frank looked at his watch.

"Seven o'clock," he said, "and I am getting hungry. Suppose we stop in the restaurant for supper. Lord Hastings will not expect us back very early."

"Suits me," said Jack.

Frank led the way and a few minutes later the two lads were seated in a cozy corner of the restaurant, gazing upon the crowd that thronged the place.

"This," said Frank, "reminds me of a night in Heligoland."

"So it does," said Jack, and added slyly: "Except that there is a certain fair singer missing."

"I had noticed that difference," said Frank. "I wonder what happened to her? I hope she did not get into trouble."

"I think she is smart enough to look out for herself," said Jack. "Some of these days, when the war is over, we may possibly encounter her some place."

"I wish we would. We owe her a whole lot."

"So we do," agreed Jack. "Now if she — —"

The lad broke off suddenly and laid a hand on his chum's arm.

"What's the matter?" demanded Frank.

For answer Jack pointed cautiously to a form at the far end of the room. The man's back was turned and he had not seen the lads.

153

"Well?" said Frank inquiringly, after glancing at the man.

"Doesn't he look familiar to you?" asked Jack.

"No; I can't say that he does — not from the back, at any rate. Whom do you think he is?"

"Well," said Jack, "I feel positive that he is none other than our old friend Count Blowinski."

"What!" exclaimed Frank incredulously. "But Count Blowinski is in Siberia by this time."

"He should be, I'll admit," agreed Jack. "But he can't be in two places, and he's here. Therefore, he can't be in Siberia."

"Pshaw!" said Frank. "Now that you have called my attention to the man I do see a certain resemblance in build, but I don't believe he is Count Blowinski."

"All right," said Jack. "But I do believe it."

Their supper was now placed before them and the lads fell to with a will, Jack the while casting an occasional glance toward the man he believed to be Count Blowinski.

Frank and Jack finished their meal before the big man — whoever he was — and Frank was for leaving immediately. But Jack protested.

"Maybe the fellow is not Count Blowinski," he said, "but it will do no harm to make sure. If I could get a look at his face, I believe I would know him whether he was disguised or not."

"Well, go over and accost him," said Frank with a smile.

"Not much," returned Jack; "for if he did happen to be the count there would be an uproar and he might get away. No, we'll wait here until he goes out and then we'll follow him."

"Good night!" said Frank. "Here you are hunting more trouble again. What would Lord Hastings say?"

"I don't know what he'd say. However, he is not here, so we won't worry about that. But if you don't want to come along, I can trail the fellow by myself."

"Oh, I'll go along," said Frank.

It was probably twenty minutes later that the man at the other end of the room rose, called for his hat and coat and made his way from the restaurant. Strain as they would, the lads were unable to catch sight of his face; so they hurried after him.

Outside, Jack recognized the figure half a block down the street. He led the way in pursuit, Frank a few paces behind.

If the man, fearing he was followed, was trying to shake off possible pursuers, he could not have gone about it in a manner more to have aroused Jack's suspicions.

First he crossed the street and then turned to the left down a side street. At the next corner he again turned to the left, walked two blocks ahead, and again turned to the left.

"Whoever he is, he's up to something with all this maneuvering," said Frank.

Jack nodded.

"I'll bet I'm right," he declared.

Again the man ahead turned a corner, this time, however, to the right. Jack and Frank came around the corner a moment later and the former uttered an exclamation of dismay. The man they had been trailing was nowhere to be seen.

"Now where do you suppose he has gone?" demanded Jack in deep disgust.

"Not knowing, I can't say," said Frank. "But it wouldn't be much of a guess to say that he disappeared in one of these houses. Which one, I haven't any idea."

"I suppose you're right," said Jack. "I wonder if he suspected he was being followed?"

"I don't believe so. I saw him turn once or twice, but I am sure he did not suspect we were trailing him."

Jack moved on.

"Here's a little alley," he called back to Frank. "Maybe he ducked in here."

"Well, take my advice and don't go fooling around there in the dark," advised Frank. "It's darker than pitch there. A man in the alley could see you, and if he were there, he'd crack your skull before you even saw him."

"Oh, I'm not going to try it," said Jack. "I was just wondering; that's all."

"As long as you stay outside and wonder, it's all right, I guess," said Frank.

But events so shaped themselves that they were not to stay out of the dark alley. Jack's sharp ears caught the sound of a body moving in the alley.

"There is some one in there," he called excitedly to Frank. "I'm going after him."

"Hold on," cried Frank. "Come back here," he added as Jack started forward.

But it was too late. Jack had already disappeared in the darkness. Drawing his revolver, Frank also sprang forward.

In the darkness it was impossible to see a hand before one, but Jack moved forward, revolver in hand, without fear.

"Who's here?" he demanded, first in French and then in German.

There was no reply, and the lad repeated the question, continuing to walk further up the dark alley.

And then, before the lad could raise a hand to prevent it, something the nature of which he could not distinguish in the brief moment before he lapsed into unconsciousness, struck him over the head. Jack fell to the ground without so much as a murmur.

There was silence again in the alley, at last broken by an exclamation from Frank, as he moved slowly forward.

"Jack! Are you all right?" he demanded.

"Jack!" exclaimed Frank again. "Are you there?"

Again there was no reply and Frank became greatly alarmed. Thinking only of his friend, and forgetful of his own safety, the lad sprang forward.

In the darkness he tripped over a prostrate form at the same moment that a blow, the exact counterpart of the one that had laid Jack low, struck him upon the head.

Frank also crumpled up without a word.

From within the darkness of the alley there came a hoarse chuckle.

"So!" exclaimed a voice that would have been familiar to both lads could they have heard it. "So! You thought to recapture Count Blowinski, eh? You fools. You should have known I would be on my guard. Now what am I going to do with them? I would like to take them with me, but I can't lug them both. I have it. I'll take one, leaving the other here."

The count stooped over the two forms which lay within a few feet of each other and lifted Jack in his arms. Then, paying no further heed to Frank, he moved toward the street.

At the mouth of the alley he hesitated for a moment. He gazed up and down the street, but saw no one. He moved on again, carrying his human burden.

Half a block from the dark alley, he mounted a pair of steps and opened a door. He glanced back over the street and saw a lone pedestrian hurrying along. Whether the man had seen him with his human burden, the count could not tell. He shrugged his shoulders and closed the door behind him.

"Well, I've got one of them here," he said to himself. "The dog! Had it not been for him my plot would not have failed. He shall pay!"

The blow which had laid Frank low in the alley had not been as severe as the one Jack had received for the reason that when Frank tripped over his friend's body, the blow had glanced off his head rather than crashing solidly upon it.

Therefore Count Blowinski, carrying Jack's limp body, had hardly passed from the alley when Frank returned to consciousness. His first thought was of Jack and he called to him. Receiving no answer, and feeling certain that there was no longer any enemy in the alley, Frank drew a match from his pocket and struck it.

The flare showed the lad that except for himself there was no human being there.

"Great Scott! He must have carried Jack away!" the lad exclaimed. "Jack would never have gone without looking for me."

Frank got quickly to his feet and hurried from the alley. Glancing in both directions, he saw a man coming toward him. The lad hurried up and accosted the man in French.

The latter shook his head, signifying that he did not understand.

Frank tried again, this time in German. The man nodded. He could understand.

"Did you see anything of two men, a man and a boy?" asked Frank.

"I saw one man," was the reply. "He seemed to be carrying another figure. Whether it was that of a man or a boy I could not tell."

"Where did he go?" demanded Frank eagerly.

"Into that house there," said the man pointing.

Frank did not waste any further words. He dashed forward, unheeding the cries of the Russian. The latter stared at the hurrying lad for some moments and then ran after him.

"The boy is going to get himself in trouble," said the Russian. "I may be able to help him."

At the foot of the steps Frank paused, for it had struck him suddenly that it would be very foolish to climb the steps and ring the bell, as he had first thought of doing. As the lad hesitated, the Russian joined him.

"What are you going to do?" he asked.

"I'm going in after my friend," replied Frank. "I was just trying to think of a way to get in without Count Blowinski being aware of my presence."

"Count Blowinski!" exclaimed the Russian.

"Yes," said Frank.

"The man who would have betrayed the Czar?"

"The same."

The Russian extended a hand to the lad.

"You may count on my help," he said.

"Good!" said Frank. "Now, we may as well try this front door. Perhaps it will open."

"If it won't, I'll open it for you," said the Russian.

They ascended the steps and Frank laid a hand on the knob and turned it cautiously. The door was locked.

"Let me get there a minute," said the Russian.

He stepped in front of Frank. Taking something from his pocket he inserted it in the keyhole. Then he stepped back as the door swung open.

Frank led the way inside. The Russian followed closely.

CHAPTER XXVII.

A FIGHT WITH A MADMAN.

When Jack came to himself he was sitting in a chair in a well lighted room. For a moment the blinding glare made it impossible for the lad to make out his surroundings, but gradually his eyes became accustomed to the light.

Before him, an evil smile on his face and a revolver in his hand, stood a large man in an attitude of leisurely nonchalance. Jack recognized Count Blowinski instantly and made a move as though to rise.

"Sit still!" commanded the count harshly.

Jack sank back in his chair. He said nothing.

"Well," said the count, "so we meet again, eh, Lieutenant Templeton? I believe that is the name, isn't it. Lieutenant Templeton."

"That is my name," said Jack.

"Well, I don't know whether it is or not. But before I am through with you it won't make much difference what your name is — perhaps I should say, was."

Jack made no reply to this threat and the count continued:

"It grieves me much that I cannot also have with us your friend and fellow-spy. I would have brought him along, but I couldn't very well carry both of you. So I chose you, because you are the largest."

"Thanks," said Jack dryly.

"Oh, well," said the count, "I'll go back when I have disposed of you. Maybe he will still be there."

"In that event," said Jack to himself, "it is up to me to play for time." Aloud he said: "Seems to me one of us should satisfy you."

"So it would, under ordinary circumstances," said the count. "But these are extraordinary circumstances. You both tricked me. Therefore you shall both pay. If I cannot find your friend when I return to hunt for him, I shall find him later."

"There is one thing that pleases me, at any rate," said Jack.

"I am glad to hear that," returned the count. "Would it be impolite for me to inquire what that one thing may be?"

"Not at all. The thing that pleases me is to know that eventually you will suffer for your treachery. The idea of a man of your kind selling out to the enemy."

"That's enough of that kind of talk," said the count angrily. "Another word like that, and I'll shoot you as you sit there."

"I can't see that the time will make any difference," said Jack quietly.

"Neither will it," was the reply. "However, I intend to use my own judgment."

"And may I ask how you intend to perform this execution?" asked Jack.

"You may," was the reply. "I intend that you shall sit in that chair. I shall move back a ways, for I want to do a little practice. It will make no difference if I do not kill you with the first shot; in fact I had rather that I did not. A little suffering won't be too great payment for what you have done."

"You are a nice sort of a gentleman, aren't you," said Jack.

"That's neither here nor there. Time was when I was a gentleman. You have made it impossible for me to continue so. That is why you must die."

"You were never a gentleman," said Jack quietly. "A gentleman is always a man of honor. You could never have been a man of honor."

"You think so, eh? Well what you think has nothing to do with matters. Are you ready to die?"

"No," said Jack. "Are you?"

"What has that to do with it?"

"A lot. I was just wondering if you would be able to meet your death as calmly as I shall be able to meet mine."

"So! a boaster, eh?"

"No, I am no boaster," said Jack.

"What are you, anyhow? An Englishman?"

"Yes. How did you guess it?"

"I have seen many of your kind. I thought so. Well, there will soon be one Englishman less in this world."

"So you say," said Jack. "To tell the truth, I'm not sure you have courage enough to shoot a man, when he is looking at you."

"You shall see."

"Of course, I know it would be easy enough for you to shoot a man in the back," said Jack. "That's about your size."

The Russian was becoming furiously angry. His face turned a deep red.

"You shall see," he said again.

"Well, why don't you shoot?" demanded Jack.

In his heart he had no doubt that the Russian would shoot. But the lad believed that if he could get the man angry enough, he could throw him off his guard for a second. Once the revolver wavered, Jack had decided to spring upon the count, come what might.

Now the count moved back another step. He raised his revolver carefully. Jack's heart sank, for there was no sign of nervousness in the man's manner. The lad was about to hurl himself forward anyhow, when there came an interruption from an unexpected source.

The door to the room suddenly burst in. Jack gave a cry of glad surprise as he saw Frank's face framed in the doorway. As his chum dashed through the door, Jack fell suddenly to the floor; and it was well that he did so, for a second later Count Blowinski's finger pressed the trigger of his revolver.

The bullet whizzed through the air right where Jack's head had been a moment before.

But the count had no time to fire again, for Frank and the Russian were upon him. Neither was armed and they dashed in close before the count could aim and fire.

Frank seized the count's revolver arm and thrust it upward. The Russian dashed in and grasped the hand that extended high in the air with the revolver. A first twist failed to dispossess the count of his weapon, but a second sharp twist had a better result. The revolver went hurling through the air, crashed through a window pane and fell to the street.

Then Count Blowinski, a powerful man, turned to give battle with his bare hands. With a sudden cry of rage, he hurled the two from him, and, stooping, seized a chair.

As his Russian opponent sprang in, the count raised the chair high in the air and brought it down on the man's head.

There was a thud as the improvised weapon struck him, and the Russian rolled on the floor. The count had successfully disposed of one of his foes. He sprang toward Frank.

The count had dropped the pieces of the chair after striking the Russian, apparently feeling able to account for Frank with his hands.

But there was one thing he seemed to have forgotten. That was Jack.

The count had not had time to watch the result of the shot when he fired at the lad and believed his bullet had gone home. When he sprang toward Frank, it was with the belief that he had a single adversary to contend with.

Therefore, he was unprepared for the attack that Jack launched from behind.

Jack, having picked himself up from the floor, had been circling around seeking a good chance at the count. He had been on the eve of jumping in when the count had seized the chair with which he disposed of the Russian, but had dropped back, unable to prevent the fall of the blow. He still felt the effects of the blow he had received in the alley, but his head was clearing fast and he was gaining strength rapidly.

Now, seeing the count advance upon Frank, Jack sprang forward.

His left hand grasped the collar of the count's coat, and checked him in his rush. As the count turned upon his new adversary, he encountered Jack's fist, which struck him squarely in the face with terrific force. The count staggered and at the same moment Jack struck again.

The second blow also went true.

Now the count recovered himself with an effort, and lowering his head, charged directly at Jack. The latter would have stepped nimbly out of the way and avoided the rush had it not been for the prostrate form of the Russian over which he tripped now. Count Blowinski threw his arms about Jack and hugged him in a tight embrace.

The breath was all but squeezed from Jack's body and it seemed that his ribs must crack. Had the count been able to retain the pressure another moment, Jack must have collapsed. Fortunately, however, the count's breath also gave out and he was forced to release his hold.

Jack sprang back gasping for breath, even as Frank leaped upon the count from behind and clasped his fingers in his throat.

With a fierce roar of rage, the count wheeled upon Frank, broke loose the lad's hold, and before Jack could come to his chum's assistance, had hurled the lad clear across the room. Frank's head struck the edge of a table with a terrible force and he dropped to the floor unconscious. Thus had the count been able to dispose of a second of his foes.

He now turned just in time to meet Jack's rush.

But Jack had decided by this time that it was foolish to close with the count, who was possessed of tremendous strength. The lad had laid his plans carefully as he was momentarily recovering from the count's last embrace. He had determined to hold his opponent off at arm's length, if possible.

For a time, it seemed that Jack would succeed. As the count came forward, Jack crouched, and sent a hard right hand blow to the count's nose. Apparently the count didn't think much of this style of fighting, for he rushed forward.

This time Jack was able to sidestep nimbly and he floored the count with a well-directed right blow just above the ear as he passed. He sprang forward to take advantage of this opening, but the count suddenly reached out and grabbed the lad by the legs.

Jack tumbled over on top of his foe.

Now both combatants threw their arms about one another and struggled for supremacy. Jack was still on top and he was determined to stay there if it were humanly possible. The count was struggling as strenuously to get from beneath Jack.

Suddenly Jack felt a finger press his cheek, missing his eye by a scant inch. Immediately Jack, by a great effort, freed himself of the other's hold, and sprang to his feet.

"Trying to gouge, eh?" muttered the lad.

It was exactly what the count had tried to do. He had been seeking Jack's eye with his finger, and he had all but found his mark.

Count Blowinski also got to his feet.

One rush he made at Jack. This, too, the lad escaped by a quick side leap, and again his fist crashed to the side of his opponent's head.

Once more the count turned and rushed and again Jack adopted the same tactics. The count staggered from the effect of the blow he received as he passed, then righted himself and seemed about to charge again.

Jack made ready to receive him.

But, so suddenly that Jack could make no move to stop him, the count turned in his tracks, leaped to the door, pulled it open and disappeared into the hall.

With a startled cry Jack leaped after him.

But when the lad reached the outside door and gazed up and down the street there was no sign of Count Blowinski.

"Now I wonder where he could have gone to," said the lad.

He gazed both ways for several minutes. Then, with a shrug of his shoulders, he turned and re-entered the house.

"He's gone," said Jack. "Now I'll see what I can do for Frank."

He ascended the stairs.

CHAPTER XXVIII.

COUNT BLOWINSKI IS CAPTURED.

"And so the count has escaped, eh?"

It was Czar Nicholas who spoke as he gazed at Jack and Lord Hastings.

"Yes, your Majesty," replied the lad, and for a second time, at the Czar's request, he went over the details of the struggle with the count.

"Well," said the Czar when the lad had concluded, "there is no telling in what part of the city he may be located now. Still, I would like to catch him. I wonder how he escaped from Siberia? or if he was ever taken?"

"Probably the latter was the case," declared Lord Hastings. "The count has been a powerful man and must have made friends. It is probable that the officer who had charge of him became temporarily blind, purposely."

"If I were sure — —" said the Czar, and he banged his fist on the table angrily.

"The first thing," said Lord Hastings, "if I may make so bold, your Majesty, is to recapture Count Blowinski before he can do any more damage."

"No small job," said the Czar.

"Perhaps not," agreed Lord Hastings. "Still it can be done."

"What would you suggest. My Lord?"

"My plan is a very simple one," said Lord Hastings, "and yet it means lots of work."

"Let's have it," said the Czar eagerly.

"Scour the city," said Lord Hastings. "Put every available man to work and search the town, every nook and corner of it. Eventually you are bound to catch him. He must be in the city still and it will be only a question of time until some of your men come upon him."

"It's a big job," said the Czar meditatively.

"And the sooner it is started the sooner the count will be taken," said Lord Hastings dryly.

"True," returned the Czar briefly. "If you will leave me now, My Lord, I shall set the wheels in motion at once."

Lord Hastings bowed, as did Jack. As they would have passed out of the Czar's presence, the latter exclaimed:

"Pray extend my condolences to your wounded second officer, My Lord. Tell him how sorry I am that he should have been injured in my service."

"It shall be done, your Majesty," replied Lord Hastings.

A moment later the commander of the D-17 and his first officer were in the street.

"Where now, sir?" asked Jack.

"To the hospital, to see how Frank is getting on," replied Lord Hastings.

They turned their steps in that direction.

When Jack had returned to Frank after his futile chase of Count Blowinski, he found his friend trying to sit up, and groaning feebly. Jack hurried to his side and raised Frank's head to his knee. An examination showed him that the back of his chum's head had been badly cut by coming in contact with the sharp table edge as he had fallen. The wound was an ugly one and Jack was much concerned.

But Frank would not hear of Jack carrying him away until he had also looked after the stranger who had so kindly come to their assistance. Jack did this and found that the man was not badly hurt. After the lad had sprinkled a little water over his face, he revived, sat up and directly got to his feet. Then he lent a helping hand in carrying Frank to the street. Here Jack stood guard while the man summoned an ambulance.

Jack climbed in the ambulance with his wounded chum and went to the hospital. The stranger declined to go along and took his departure. At the hospital, Jack saw his friend made comfortable, learned from the attending physician that the wound was not dangerous, and then hastened to report to Lord Hastings.

Lord Hastings was much put out to learn that Frank had been hurt and he upbraided Jack for putting their lives in jeopardy. Nevertheless, he realized the gravity of the fact that Count Blowinski was again at large and had hurriedly sought an audience with the Czar, where we found the two British officers at the opening of this chapter.

They were admitted to the hospital immediately and the nurse told them they could see Frank if he were not sleeping. She was gone a few moments and returned with the information that he was awake and anxious to see them. The two made their way to Frank's side quickly.

Frank smiled feebly as Lord Hastings sat down on the side of the bed and took his hand.

"How do you feel?" demanded the commander gravely.

Frank smiled a trifle at the apparent anxiety of his commander. His head was swathed in bandages and he looked almost ludicrous.

"Well, I don't feel like going for a joy ride," he replied with an attempt at levity, "but I could feel a whole lot worse."

"Head pain you much?" asked Lord Hastings.

"No, sir; not much. I know I've got a hole there, but it doesn't feel like a very big one. Pretty sharp table in the count's house, sir."

"It must have been, to lay you out like that," agreed Lord Hastings.

"If it hadn't been for that, I would have been in at the finish," said Frank. "By the way, have you discovered any trace of the count?"

"Not yet; but by this time the Czar has given orders to scour the city and it is only a question of time until the count is apprehended."

"I hope they get him, sir; and still, I would like to be there when they do."

"You won't be," declared Lord Hastings grimly. "From present indications you will be here for the next three or four days. After this I am going to keep a closer eye on you. You two are too valuable officers for the king to lose; and that's just what will happen unless I tie a string to you."

"Oh, I guess you won't do that, sir," smiled Frank. "You wouldn't like to be tied down, sir. Neither do we."

"Well, perhaps I won't do quite that bad," said Lord Hastings; "but I am free to tell you that right now that is just exactly what I feel like doing."

The conversation was continued for some moments longer; in fact, until the nurse approached and told Lord Hastings and Jack that they had talked long enough and that she would have her patient kept awake no longer.

Frank protested at first, but Lord Hastings silenced him.

"If you don't keep quiet," he said, "we won't be permitted to see you to-morrow."

"I'll be quiet then and go to sleep," Frank decided.

Lord Hastings and Jack took their leave and made their way to the quarters in the palace placed at their disposal by command of the Czar himself. Ten minutes after their arrival there they were abed and fast asleep.

It seemed that they had hardly closed their eyes when they were awakened by a loud rapping at the door. Both were on their feet instantly, and Lord Hastings called out:

"Well?"

"His Majesty's compliments, sir, and he would like to have you come to him at once—both of you," came a voice from without.

"Tell His Majesty that we shall obey his summons instantly," Lord Hastings made reply.

There came the sound of footsteps retreating down the hall.

"Wonder what the Czar wants, sir?" asked Jack excitedly, as he dressed.

"I haven't any idea," returned his commander. "But certainly it must be something important for him to summon us thus in the middle of the night."

Jack looked at his watch.

"Quarter after one, sir," he said. "Yes, it must be something important." He paused, struck by a sudden thought. "By Jove, sir! Maybe Count Blowinski has been captured."

"Pshaw!" said Lord Hastings. "That is hardly possible. They can't have been looking for him more than a couple of hours."

"And still that may be it, sir."

"Oh yes, it may be, but I don't think so."

But as it developed Jack's guess had been correct.

For, when they were ushered into the Czar's presence once more, the first figure upon which their eyes rested was that of the count himself.

"By Jove! you were right," said Lord Hastings in an aside to Jack.

The lad smiled but said nothing aloud. To himself, however, he remarked:

"Another of those things Frank calls hunches."

The Czar greeted them with a smile. In spite of the lateness of the hour, the Czar was as fully dressed as when they left him earlier in the night and he had the appearance of not having retired.

"My Lord and Mr. Templeton," said the Czar, "I see that you have recognized our friend in the corner there."

Lord Hastings and Jack nodded and the Czar continued:

"We were fortunate enough to come upon him almost at once; and I'll wager, My Lord, that you have no idea where we found him."

The Czar paused, apparently awaiting an answer. Lord Hastings shook his head.

"No, your Majesty, I haven't the slightest idea," he returned.

"Well," said the Czar, "what will you say when I tell you that the good count was caught in the act of trying to break into the palace?"

"Into the palace!" repeated Lord Hastings in the greatest surprise.

"Exactly," returned the Czar with a smile. "It seems that he had still further designs on my life. Am I not right, my dear Count?"

He turned to Count Blowinski with a pleasant smile on his features.

The count glowered at him angrily.

"Yes, it's true," he shouted. "And if you weren't so cowardly that you keep yourself so well guarded, I would have reached you. I have not given up hope yet."

"Then you may as well, Count," was the reply. "After this morning at daybreak, I promise you you will worry about me no more. As Siberia is too small to hold you, I must take other means to insure my own safety. No, Count, after this night you will trouble no one."

The count growled under his breath, but he made no audible response to the Czar's words, although he must have realized what the Russian monarch meant.

"Now," said the Czar, "I wouldn't be surprised if the count would tell us just how he managed to escape from Siberia—the bourne from which a traveler seldom returneth. I am curious."

"I shall tell you nothing," declared the count decidedly.

"Come, come, Count!" exclaimed His Majesty. "Surely you will not be so selfish. On my word, I am curious to know. Pray enlighten my curiosity."

Count Blowinski looked at the Czar long and earnestly; and at last he replied with a shrug of his shoulders:

"Oh, well, I cannot see that it will make much difference. It will get one of your most trusted officers into trouble, but he is loyal to you, so I should be glad to implicate him. In the first place, then, I never went to Siberia."

"As I expected," Lord Hastings interrupted.

"Continue," said the Czar.

"Very well. The officer in whose command I was placed chanced to be an old friend—a young man, rather, who had served under me and had come to think of me highly."

"The more fool he," the Czar interrupted.

"So you may think. At any rate, he did not believe the charges against me, apparently plain though they were. I played upon his credulity to such an extent that he at last agreed to allow me to escape."

"As I suspected," Lord Hastings interrupted a second time; and a second time the Czar exclaimed:

"Continue, Count."

"It was easily arranged," the count went on. "One night, while the camp slept, this officer came to my prison tent—we had not yet started for Siberia—unbound me, gave me one of his own uniforms and permitted me to go free. I walked out boldly and without being accosted. I immediately left Moscow and came to St. Petersburg—I should say Petrograd—where I have remained unrecognized until I was seen by these two English upstarts in a restaurant to-night. That is all there is to the story."

"Plainly and briefly told, Count," said the Czar approvingly. "You may be pleased to know, perhaps, that you shall leave my Empire as quickly and as satisfactorily."

"You mean?" questioned the count, raising an eyebrow.

"Exactly," replied the Czar significantly. "In the morning at daybreak."

Count Blowinski shrugged his shoulders disdainfully.

"I am not afraid," he said quietly.

"No," returned the Czar. "To your credit, I am glad to say that for you. You have been my friend, and in spite of the manner in which you have betrayed me, I am glad to know that you are not a coward. I hope you shall bear up bravely under the ordeal."

"You need have no fear," said the count with a bow.

"Good," said the Czar.

He signaled the officer of the guard in charge of the prisoner. "Take him away!" he exclaimed. "Guard him carefully and at daybreak to-morrow—I should say this morning—take a squad, of soldiers, stand the count against the wall and shoot him. It is time he was put out of the way."

Then Count Blowinski did a sudden and audacious thing. At the Czar's last words, and before any man present could raise a hand to stop him, the count leaped forward; and as he did so his hand dropped to his belt.

CHAPTER XXIX.

DEATH OF THE TRAITOR—OLD ENGLAND AGAIN.

Czar Nicholas shrank back.

In the hand of Count Blowinski, which flashed aloft above his head, a knife gleamed in the light. A cry of horror went up from those in that part of the room who were so far back as to preclude a possibility of their being able to interfere in time to save the Emperor.

Those closer to the Czar hurled themselves forward; but they had hesitated a moment when the count sprang forward and they too would have been too late.

In all that room, among the score of officers and soldiers, there was only a single soul who had the presence of mind, the courage and the alertness to act in time.

Jack sprang forward.

In spite of the fact that Count Blowinski had seemed, apparently, resigned to his fate, there was something in the man's eye that had warned Jack and told him to be on his guard.

Even as he leaped Jack knew he was taking a desperate chance. The thought flashed through his mind that even he would be too late to save the Czar. But there was not a moment of hesitation; not a second of indecision on his part.

Straight between the Czar and Count Blowinski Jack sprang, at the same time raising a hand to catch the upraised arm, the hand of which grasped the knife in a firm grip.

But in his haste the lad had not gauged the distance accurately. True he had interposed his body between that of the Czar and the would-be assassin, but he failed to grasp the upraised arm.

The moment that he realized he had missed, Jack swerved a bit, and the knife, descending, slashed his right shoulder. Had he not swerved it had been his heart.

Before Count Blowinski could move to strike again, Jack, whirling suddenly, seized the arm in his left hand and clung to it tightly, his now useless right arm hanging by his side.

The Czar was safe.

With a cry of baffled rage, Count Blowinski gave a desperate wrench and freed himself from the lad's grasp.

With his eyes red with rage, he again raised the knife and cried out at Jack:

"Now die!"

The knife descended, but even as it would have found its mark, it fell clattering to the floor as a revolver shot rang out.

Once, twice, Count Blowinski spun round on his heel, made a desperate effort to keep his feet; then plunged to the floor on his face.

There was a breathless silence in the room as Jack moved forward, turned the count over on his back and laid a hand over his heart. Then he looked up and said quietly:

"He's dead."

The lad got to his feet and turned to Lord Hastings, who still held a smoking revolver in his hand — it was he who had fired the shot that had saved Jack's life.

"You, sir — —" he began, then staggered, and before Lord Hastings could raise a hand to catch him, pitched forward across the body of the count.

Instantly the Czar became greatly excited. He waved his arms above his head and cried out:

"Summon my physician immediately! Hurry! What is the matter with you? Can't you see this lad is in need of immediate assistance? My physician! Quickly!"

Instantly all became confusion. Men rushed out the door, treading upon each other's feet and jostling one another furiously in their effort to obey the Czar's command.

175

Lord Hastings and the Czar sprang to Jack's side at the same moment, but it was the Russian ruler who raised the lad's head to his knee and placed a hand over the heart.

The effort was rewarded by a slight beating.

"He lives!" cried the Czar. "Some water quickly!"

Lord Hastings sprang to obey this command and soon the Czar himself was bathing Jack's face and talking to him, as would a father to a son who was ill.

And at last Jack opened his eyes.

The Czar breathed a sigh of great relief.

"Thank God!" he exclaimed fervently.

Lord Hastings also now stooped over Jack.

"How do you feel, Jack?" he asked anxiously.

Jack smiled up at him feebly.

"Shoulder hurts considerably, sir," he replied, and winced with the pain. "Foolish of me to topple over like this, though, sir."

"Foolish!" repeated the Czar, and then sprang to his feet and exclaimed excitedly:

"My doctor! My doctor! Where is he? Doesn't the man have sense enough to hurry? By my soul, I'll have him sent to Siberia if he is not here in two minutes!"

And His Majesty continued to rave until a few moments later a little man hurried in briskly.

"Where have you been?" exclaimed the Czar. "Don't you know enough to hurry when I send for you? See to this boy at once. At once, do you hear?"

The physician paid no attention to the Emperor of all the Russians more than to push His Majesty aside as he said shortly:

"Stand back, now, all of you and give me room."

Not another man was there in all the empire who could speak to the Czar like that.

He took no heed of any of those standing about, except to give an occasional order as he worked; and after ten minutes he looked up at the Czar and said:

"There is no danger, sire."

"Thank God!" exclaimed the Czar again. "I will not have him die. He shall have the best that the Empire affords. Have him taken to my own suite immediately."

And the Czar would hear of nothing else. Lord Hastings he commanded to be his guest in the palace and the latter could do naught but comply.

And so, for the next three days, Jack lay ill in the Czar's palace. Daily he grew stronger, for he was of a vigorous and healthy constitution and after the first day there was absolutely no danger.

It was a dismal time for Lord Hastings, who now had both of his officers on the sick list; and the commander of the D-17 divided his time between the sick room in the Czar's palace and the hospital, where Frank was confined.

But at last the time came when the physician decided that Jack could get up and move about a little. This was indeed welcome news to Jack, who insisted, the first day he was out of bed, upon being taken to see Frank.

"Well," said Frank, as he greeted his chum with outstretched hand, "it seems that if I get into a little trouble, you must do likewise."

"That's not the reason I did it," was the reply. "Say, we're a couple of fine officers for King George, aren't we? We're always in trouble of some kind. The first thing you know, he'll be asking for our resignations."

"Oh, I guess not," said Lord Hastings, who had overheard this remark. "However, I am greatly afraid that I am going to lose you both."

"Going to lose us?" repeated Jack in surprise.

"What do you mean, sir?" demanded Frank anxiously.

"Why," said Lord Hastings, "I shall have to report your conduct to His Majesty, King George, and when I do — — "

"I told you," broke in Jack. "His Majesty will ask us to resign."

"By George! I hope not," exclaimed Frank.

"And when I do," continued Lord Hastings, not heeding the interruptions, "I shall probably lose you both, for His Majesty probably will take you away from me."

"What for, sir?" demanded Jack.

"Why," was the reply, "His Majesty will realize, as I have long ago, that you are too valuable officers to be fooling around as lieutenants. You will probably get the promotions you both deserve."

Jack and Frank fell suddenly silent. They had thought of nothing like this. But after some moments Frank said:

"Well, sir, if there is any danger of such a catastrophe, I hope that you will be kind enough to say nothing to the king."

"Frank is right, sir," agreed Jack. "It would indeed be a catastrophe."

"It would be a catastrophe for me if I were to lose you," said Lord Hastings very quietly.

As the days passed the injuries of both lads healed rapidly. At the end of a week both were feeling perfectly fit and each expressed his earnest desire to put to sea again.

"Not until you are absolutely fit," was Lord Hastings' decision. "You must remember that we face a dangerous task passing through the Kiel Canal on the way home and I want you both to be absolutely in ship-shape before I attempt it."

"We've gone through three times now," said Jack quietly. "I guess we can manage it once more."

"And going back," said Lord Hastings, "we shall go as we came this last time — with no stops and no thought of engaging a single one of the enemy."

"But, sir — —" began Frank.

"There are no 'buts' in this case," declared Lord Hastings with finality. "I'm the commander of the D-17, and what I say goes, if I have to put you both in irons to keep you quiet."

When Lord Hastings took this tone, both lads knew there was no use of arguing the matter; and while both felt they would like to strike another blow at the German fleet on their homeward journey, they were forced to accept Lord Hastings' dictum.

At length the day for leaving came; but before they could go aboard the D-17, at the Czar's command, they needs must dine with him. This they did, and in the presence of the many notables who sat down to table, the Czar, following the feast, arose and complimented each lad separately and highly.

And he closed with this injunction:

"If, at any time, during the war or after peace has come to bless our several lands, you should chance to be in Russia, either of you, and you fail to come to me before another, I promise you that I shall seek you out and have you sent to Siberia for life — that I may see you whenever I lose my sense of what is right and wrong and need something to set me right."

The Czar finished his remarks amid tremendous applause, much to the embarrassment of the two lads, who stood there, faces flushed and grinning foolishly. But the banquet came to an end at last and Lord Hastings, Frank and Jack took their departure, the praises of the Czar still ringing in their ears.

They went aboard the D-17 the same night and made ready for their departure in the morning.

And as the D-17 steamed slowly along on the surface the following morning, what a terrible din and roar there was, as every Russian ship of war in the harbor fired a farewell salute!

Said Lord Hastings to his two officers:

"You may live many, many years, but it will be long ere you will have the honors heaped upon you that you have earned in Russia."

There was no reply that either lad could make, so they stood silently on the bridge, watching the city of Petrograd disappear in the distance; and presently they came once more to the broad expanse of the Baltic.

The journey back to the shores of old England was without a single incident to mar its peacefulness. They passed through the Kiel Canal without going to the surface, nor were they disturbed by a foe in the depths. The mines they steamed by safely also, and soon they once more found themselves under the protection of the great British fleet.

Lord Hastings immediately ran for London; and six hours after the D-17 had docked there, the lads found themselves once more in Lord Hastings' palatial home. And Lady Hastings took them both by the arms and addressed them thus:

"You know how fond I have grown of you two boys. You have been away long and I have missed you. This time, I shall keep you with me."

As Frank and Jack blushed and bowed and scraped uncomfortably, Lord Hastings only smiled and nodded.

"Yes," said Lady Hastings quietly, "you have done much for England, all three of you boys," and she glanced affectionately at her husband. "Now, for a time, you shall take orders from no one but me. You shall all stay here and rest!"

THE END.

Milton Keynes UK
Ingram Content Group UK Ltd.
UKHW010643031023
429856UK00004B/247

9 791041 950546